Villere House

Blood of My Blood

C.D. Hussey Leslie Fear

ACKNOWLEDGMENTS

From Leslie:

To my lovely husband, Randy, for his continued support and patience while I wrote, edited, emailed, took over his computer for more days than I should have and everything else I'm sure I tortured him with. I love you, honey, "all the way to the barn and back!"

To my Mom, Sue Colburn, for her unending elation and for, (I'm sure), showing off every single thing related to our book. Your excitement was palpable and I love you even more for it!

To my dear friend, Stephenie Thomas for putting up with my phone calls while I power-walked, got ready in the mornings or just wanted to chat with a truly honest and awesome, supportive friend. I love you to pieces!

To Morgan Parker for your praise of my writing. You turned out to be a reliable source in this business who didn't blow smoke, only the insightful truth. I will be eternally grateful!

To The Dean's List Facebook group. Your continuous encouragement, helpful suggestions and awesome cheerleading will never be forgotten. Thank you from the bottom of my heart.

To my co-author, Carla, for taking me and my story on. You called me out, made me think, stayed honest and because of that, you mentored me into a better writer. Words can never fully express my gratitude. I think you're rock star...seriously!

From Carla:

A big thanks to Leslie for bringing me into this project and letting me run with it. And for putting up with me and my quirks. Obviously, I couldn't have done it without you.

From Leslie and Carla:

We would also like to take this opportunity to thank our beta-readers: Stephenie Thomas, Sarah Phelps, Tami Fairley, Tashia Brandenburg, Laura Wilson, Beth Rustenhaven, Vanessa Proehl, Tosha Khoury, Keelie Lington, Jennifer Lawson and Jule Delgado.

Your time, insightful comments and helpful suggestions were priceless! We are grateful beyond words!

To Michelle Warren who so wonderfully designed our awesome book cover. You listened and gave us exactly what we wanted, and on the first try! It was so incredibly easy to work with you as you went above and beyond so many times. We appreciate everything you did for us!

And finally, Carla and I would like to thank the lovely author, Tracey Garvis-Graves for her kind, thoughtful and amazing comments about our story. Your encouragement meant the world!

CHAPTER ONE

Light rain began to fall, saturating the already damp air with so much moisture it felt thick. Élise quickened her pace, tucking her chin until her bonnet shielded her face from the drizzle.

Clutching her basket close, she hustled down the walk, carefully avoiding puddles. Her boots were due to be resoled but she was hoping to push the expense back until fall—after the cotton crop had been harvested and her investments paid off. If she had the boots resoled now, she might be forced to borrow money.

Perhaps she was being overly cautious, but thus far, debt was an evil she'd been lucky to avoid. When he died, Nathanael had left her with a healthy estate. The last thing she wanted to do was mismanage it.

Even though he'd been gone more than three years now, the prospect of single-handedly running a household and caring for her children was still a daunting and frightening task. She might have become overly frugal, but better to be frugal than a widow with no money.

She normally wouldn't venture out in such

weather, but her errands were somewhat urgent and Rosette was busily fixing dinner. Maintaining only one servant meant she often had to tend to mundane chores herself. She didn't mind, but it was much different than the privileged life she'd lived with Nathanael.

The rain tapered off to a fine mist as she rounded the corner onto Rue Dumaine and she slowed her pace to something more comfortable. The streets empty, her shoes clicked loudly in the quiet.

The sound of drums joined her footsteps. She couldn't quite tell where it might be coming from, but it seemed like it was no more than a block away. Quiet at first, it built in volume and intensity as she walked until it seemed like it was right next to her.

She slowed her pace even more, curious to discover the source.

Pausing at an ivy covered wrought iron gate buried in a thick brick wall, she strained to locate the drums. They were coming from inside the gated wall, she was sure of it.

The rhythm was so foreign. And the drums...they were nothing like she'd ever heard. Not like the crisp notes of a marching band drum, these sounded deep, rich, earthy.

She looked down the street in either direction. Not a soul in sight. But it was wrong to peep...

She started to walk forward, away from the gate, and then paused again as the drum rhythm intensified even more, becoming frenzied, almost spastic. Chanting joined the drums. It wasn't exactly singing, it was more guttural and in a language she didn't know. Élise spoke French, Spanish and some English. This reminded her of the dialect she heard spoken by slaves when they first stepped off the ships from

Africa.

Now she had to know what was going on in that courtyard. She'd pray for forgiveness later.

Peeling back the curtain of ivy a few inches, she peered through the opening. Two men and a woman sat in a semi-circle around a small open fire. Wooden goblet drums pinched between their knees, they pounded ferociously on them while another woman chanted and danced. She wore only a thin chemise that was soaked with either water or sweat and was now completely sheer. Her long, curly black hair floated around her face like the tendrils of smoke twisting up from the fire she danced around.

Élise immediately realized she was spying on a Voodoo ritual. She knew she had no business watching, but couldn't seem to look away. Enthralled by the woman's supple, animal-like grace, Élise watched in a trancelike state as she dipped two fingers into a bowl and smeared red paint on her face.

Or possibly blood.

Just then, the woman turned and looked directly at her, the drums and chanting coming to an abrupt stop. For one terrifying moment their gazes locked. The red liquid dripped down her nose and over her full lips, and her eyes, hateful and angry, looked completely black, devoid of any white, not even a hint.

Élise jerked away from the gate, keeping her eyes fixed on it as she scurried backward. When twenty feet of distance separated her from the closed gate, she finally turned.

And ran right into something large and firm.

She screamed, her basket falling onto the walk, the contents scattering. Large hands steadied her. "Easy," a deep voice urged without a hint of malice.

She glanced at the hands. Definitely male, they

were a rich caramel color and completely encircled her arms, even with the thick sleeves of her coat. Her eyes slowly drifted up, taking in the stranger's fine wool coat, noting the solid silver buttons, the quality of silk of his red vest, and the tightly woven linen cravat.

The face attached to the body was no less striking than the expensive clothing. The same caramel skin covered a square jaw, high cheekbones, and a strong nose that was more Indian than African. His lips were full and soft looking and curled up in a friendly smile. And his eyes...deep, dark brown, and focused on her with gentle concern.

Her fear cast aside, she was momentarily swept away by his exotic beauty and the strength in his hands as he supported her. With a brief shake of her head to clear it, she righted her body, gently pulling away. "I'm sorry. I didn't see you—"

"No need to apologize. Here, let me help you." He stooped and began retrieving the fallen items and returning them to her basket. When he reached the bottle of calomel he frowned. "Are you ill?"

"No, not me. My daughter. It's nothing." She waved it off after his frown deepened. "She's merely feeling a little lethargic and the doctor suggested we purge her."

He glanced at the bottle again, his frown deepening even more until the groove between his black brows was a deep crevice. "How old is your daughter?" he asked as he placed the bottle in her basket.

"Three."

His eyes grew dark and serious. "Be careful with that." He gestured toward the medicine.

She wasn't sure what he meant by the statement.

4

Calomel was what the doctor recommended. It wasn't always a pleasant medicine, but it was necessary.

"I will." She pulled the basket close. "Thank you for your assistance."

He tipped his hat. "My pleasure."

Looking toward the ground and away from his beautiful gaze, she hurried down the road. Before crossing the street, she quickly glanced back. Standing in the same spot the tall stranger continued to watch her. And just beyond at the wrought iron gate stood the woman from the ritual—still wearing nothing more than a shift. Her eyes were focused on Élise with undeniable hostility that could be felt one hundred feet away.

Feeling the color drain from her face, she immediately turned and hustled away.

"Lottie. Lottie!"

Two fingers snapped in front of her face, drawing her out of the memory of the weirdest dream she'd ever experienced. It had been playing over and over again in her mind since she woke up. So vivid, so real...it wasn't even like a dream, it was more like a memory.

In the dream, she *was* Élise, walking down the rainy, 19th century New Orleans streets, seeing the world through *her* eyes.

The details Lottie remembered were so crisp. She couldn't imagine how she could possibly know them. She was a social-psych major, not a history major. But somehow she knew every small detail of Élise's boots. And calomel? What the hell was calomel?

"What's up with you?" Amanda wondered.

"You've been spaced out all morning."

"Just hung over." It wasn't exactly a lie. Charlotte, or Lottie as everyone called her, was hung over. And rightly so. It had been non-stop Daiquiris and Hand Grenades since they stepped off the plane yesterday. The previous evening was actually a blur and the pile of beads covering the coffee table in their hotel suite had her a little worried. They were in New Orleans though, so…

She wondered if going to bed drunk had been the fuel for the bizarre dream. Maybe she was channeling some long lost history lesson or book she'd read and promptly forgotten. She'd read a book a week since she was twelve. That was a lot of books to forget.

"Ugh, tell me about it."

Lottie glanced over at her other friend, the third in their New Orleans spring break trio. Samantha was slumped in her chair, sunglasses pulled tight over her face even though the Café du Monde patio was covered. Sam didn't raise her head when she spoke. She kept her eyes glued to the phone in her hand, fingers clicking away furiously in spite of her pallor complexion. Her coffee and beignet remained untouched on the table.

Amanda snatched the phone.

At that, Sam came to life. "Hey! I need that!"

"For what?"

"I have fans…"

Amanda rolled her eyes. "This is spring-fucking-break. Take a break. Literally."

Sam reached for the phone and for an irritating couple of seconds, they were like two little kids fighting over a ball on the playground.

"So, what's the game plan today?" Lottie interjected, grabbing the phone from Amanda and

6

handing it back to Sam. She felt like their mom. Someone needed to intervene and of course, *she* would be the voice of reason. She always seemed to be the voice of reason. And not always by choice.

She felt like that often—being the mom part. They might all be the same age, twenty-two, but Lottie felt decades older than her college friends. She supposed it made sense since she'd pretty much been on her own since she was fifteen. Sure, she'd drifted through a few foster homes, but nurturing was hardly a phrase that described them.

"I say we chill by the pool with some Daiquiris," Amanda offered.

Just the thought of a Daiquiri made her stomach turn. "God, how can you think about alcohol right now?"

"Ever heard of hair of the dog?"

"That doesn't really work," she said. "It just delays the hangover."

Sam finally put her phone away. "Jesus, Lottie, sometimes you are such a prude. Poolside Daiquiris sound awesome. There are some seriously hot guys at the hotel I wouldn't mind getting to know." She stood up. "Let's get the eff out of here."

Lottie looked at her untouched food. "Shouldn't you eat something…"

"Good grief." Sam snatched up the beignet, took a bite, powdered sugar raining down on the table, and then took a healthy drink of coffee. She made a face. "Ugh. The coffee tastes like dirt."

"That's the chicory." Amanda rose too. "Hey, I saw a place on the way advertising frozen Irish coffees. Wouldn't mind stopping for one."

"Sounds delish."

Actually, to Lottie, it sounded like the beginning

of a very long day.

Pigeons hustled to get out of their way as they picked their way through the crowded patio crammed with full tables. At the entrance, a line twice as long as the one they'd endured earlier now extended past a saxophone player belting out jazz tunes, almost reaching the traffic light on the corner.

It seemed incredibly warm for March, but they were coming from northern Missouri so anything above freezing felt warm. Sun poured from a cloudless sky as they trekked down the busy street and within minutes, Lottie had to remove her light jacket.

Walking through the slow moving tourists was like swimming in molasses. Sam and Amanda were obviously in a hurry and shoved their way through the crowd, linking hands to make a single-file chain. Lottie wasn't sure what they were hurrying to, but she didn't argue when Amanda reached back and grabbed her hand. If she argued every time their behavior baffled her, she'd never know peace.

The bar with the frozen Irish coffees wasn't far, probably not more than five hundred feet from Café du Monde, but it took them almost five minutes to get there. Luckily, the bar was much less crowded than the streets. Probably a good thing for the livers in New Orleans, since it wasn't yet noon. The tattooed bartender with the Betty Page bangs quickly filled their order—three cocktails even though Lottie insisted she didn't want one—and they were back on their way.

Once off the packed street of Decatur, they were able to pick up a more reasonable pace. The streets became quiet, almost peaceful. Her surroundings seemed familiar, but she shrugged it off to the fact that most of the streets in the French Quarter looked the same and they'd traveled down many the day before.

As they walked past the door to one of the few shops dotting the quiet street, she felt an unsettling tug—like desire to look over at a neighboring car while driving on the highway only to discover the other person is looking at you. She paused. Amanda and Sam didn't seem to notice and kept walking.

It didn't surprise her. She was often the third wheel. She'd only become friends with Amanda because they'd roomed together in the dorms for two years. She was pretty sure they kept her around mostly out of some weird dorm loyalty. She didn't party like they did, didn't hook up with guys like they did... Sam was right; she could be a bit of a prude. At least compared to them.

"*Villere House of Voodoo*," was carved into a large wooden sign that hung over the door. She peered through the dingy window into the cluttered shop. It didn't look much different than the other Voodoo shops they'd passed—crammed full of masks, statues, Voodoo dolls, beads, incense, oils, bottles filled most likely with herbs... Still, she felt strangely compelled to go inside.

Her thoughts drifted to her dream. The woman in the courtyard, writhing in a sweat-soaked dress around a fire while drummers banged out a heady beat. Those black eyes...they'd been so hate-filled.

She shuddered involuntarily.

You're an idiot, she told herself. It was a dream. Nothing more. Probably brought on by whatever drink was in the cup with the plastic skull on it at that Voodoo themed bar Amanda puked in last night.

"Hey," Amanda's voice cut through her thoughts. "You comin'?"

Lottie glanced up. The girls were standing twenty

feet away, waiting…impatiently. She looked back at the sign that was somehow weathered and well crafted at the same time. The weathering had to have been done on purpose. Some of these shops seemed so hokey.

"I want to check this place out."

Sam groaned and Amanda's tone didn't sound any more enthusiastic. "Let's do it later," she said. "My drink's melting."

Lottie glanced at the store. Even though they'd be in New Orleans for several more days, she felt like she had to go inside now. Not tomorrow and definitely not the next day. It was like something wanted her to enter the store. Insisting was more like it.

"You guys go back to the hotel. I'll catch up in a few."

"What are you gonna do with your drink?"

Why Amanda cared she wasn't drinking was beyond Lottie. "Here," she jogged over to Amanda and handed her the frozen coffee. "I'm not going to drink this."

"You sure?"

"Yep, knock yourself out. I'm pretty sure I've still got plenty of alcohol in my system."

Amanda shrugged. Now two-fisting it, she asked, "You sure you can find the hotel?"

Lottie grinned at her. "I'm the one who found it last night."

"That's true," Sam said from behind Amanda. Her body was already turned the other direction and Lottie could tell she was even more anxious than Amanda to get moving. "If we'd kept following you," Sam said to her, "we would've been sleeping by the river with the rats and homeless guys."

"Whatever. Hey, we'll see you in a few then."

Lottie didn't bother watching them saunter down the street. She turned and headed straight for the Voodoo shop, the compulsion to go in even stronger. Why? She had no idea. But the weirdness of the situation was enough reason for her to want to find out.

CHAPTER TWO

The creak of the heavy wooden door when she pushed it open overwhelmed the delicate ring of the door chime. She cringed at the sound, like she was sneaking back into her room after curfew. Which was silly because no one seemed to notice.

A mixture of aromas greeted her when she stepped inside—Nag Champa and Sage and possibly Sandalwood. At least a half-dozen people milled about, making the room feel even smaller. The house was clearly old, with crown molding that looked grand in its thickness and window glass that waved from imperfection.

She made her way along the perimeter, taking in the wares as she passed. Nothing was all that compelling. The Voodoo dolls were cute, but they were sold at every T-shirt shop on every corner of every street. Other than the dolls and African art, it really didn't seem much different than a run-of-the-mill head shop.

There was an altar in the corner...

She made her way to it, squeezing behind a couple reading the back of a jar—probably some sort of sex potion based on the way they were giggling—and shelves filled with merchandise.

Sitting on a small, cloth-covered table was a strange statue, beads dripping from its arms and legs and whatever horn things adorned its head. On the wall behind it hung a cross with skulls carved into the wood, a serpent climbing the stipes. Surrounding the statue were candles in glass containers and baskets filled with coins and candy and small bottles of liquor. A portrait of a woman, also donning strands of colorful beads, joined the statue.

Lottie bent to get a better look at her. She was beautiful, with impossibly dark eyes that contrasted beautifully with her light, honey-colored skin. It might have only been a painting, but the eyes seemed so lifelike, so real, so…hateful.

It was the woman from her dream. The woman in the courtyard.

"May I help you?"

With a startled scream, Lottie jumped backward, running into the shelves behind her. "Oh my God!" she exclaimed, one hand clutched to her chest and the other trying to steady a row of candles rocking dangerously on the shelf.

The arm of the man who'd startled her jerked forward, reaching across her to help keep the inventory where it belonged. He was tall, so his chest passed in front of her and she had to look up to get a glimpse of his face.

Oh. My.

He was hot, sexy hot, kinda like a twenty-something Johnny Depp with darker skin, fuller lips, and a stronger jaw. He even had similar hair, thick black hair worn long enough to be haphazardly tousled. And his eyes...so dark they were almost black. Whatever essential oil he was wearing wafted over. Earthy, musky, and slightly sweet. It smelled amazing.

She laughed off her clumsiness. "Sorry about that. You scared me. My mind's on overdrive today."

"No worries. Nothing's broken." His deep, rich voice was laced with an accent identifying him as a New Orleans native—that strange mix of South meets East Coast. "Can I help you with anything?"

"Ah, well..." When the question was raised she wasn't sure how to respond. What did she want? Why *was* she here? Oh, right, because she'd be *drawn* in.

She resisted the urge to roll her eyes at her own thoughts.

"Who is that?" she asked instead, pointing to the portrait of the woman she'd swear had been in her dreams.

He didn't so much as glance at the portrait. His dark eyes were fixated on her, studying her with quiet scrutiny. "That is Sanite Villere, one of the lesser known Voodoo Queens of the early nineteenth century." The response sounded scripted, like he said it one hundred times per day. He probably did.

"Really?" She stared at the painting again. The eyes had lost the striking realism and seething hatred from earlier. It was now just a painting of a beautiful Creole woman, nothing more, nothing less. Obviously it *had* been nothing more than her imagination.

"So they say. Most people have only heard of Marie Laveau, but there were many priests and priestesses in New Orleans' Voodoo past." He opened his hands, gesturing around the room. "This was her house. We lost it for a while after the Civil War, but the Villere family was able to reclaim it thirty years ago."

She really liked watching him talk. Besides his obvious amazing looks, he had this calm confidence that simply oozed from him.

"We? So I take it you're a Villere?"

"Yeah, Xavier Villere."

That explained the eyes. His were very similar to the painter's rendition of Sanite's. Well, minus the hate. Not that it was there now.

"That's really cool," she said, shaking off the memory. "It must be amazing to have such a rich family history." And know about it, she added silently.

She had no family. Zero, zilch, nada. No parents or siblings. No grandparents or aunts or uncles. Not even any cousins. Her parents died long before she cared to ask about her family history and now there was no one to ask. It somehow made her feel even more isolated and alone than if she'd just been an orphan.

"I suppose."

The nonchalant way he shrugged off such a rich heritage had her perplexed. She wasn't so dramatic to say she'd give anything to delve into her past, but she'd give quite a bit. To understand where she came from... Maybe it would help her understand where she was going.

"Was there something specific you were looking for?" he asked.

Right, because he was a clerk in a Voodoo shop. It wasn't like they were friends chatting it up on a beautiful Friday afternoon. Or that he was flirting with her.

"Um..." She glanced around at the shelves of merchandise. She could easily say she was just looking but that somehow seemed wrong. Maybe she should grab a couple Voodoo dolls and head back to the hotel and join Amanda and Sam by the pool.

"You know, I'd love a basic book on New Orleans Voodoo," she said. "Do you have anything like that?"

"Of course." He led her over to a bookshelf filled with books on every topic from Voodoo to African folklore to spells and curses. He handed her a thin paperback with a picture of Marie Laveau on the glossy cover. "If you want something simple, I think this one's pretty good. And it covers New Orleans."

"Anything about Sanite?"

"Not yet," another man in his late-twenties interjected. He emerged from a beaded curtain leading to a dark room where Lottie could just make out the edge of another altar. He was tall like Xavier, with the striking good looks that hinted of a Native American as well as African heritage. But that was where the similarities ended. Where Xavier had thick black hair, skin the color of coffee and cream, and eyes so dark they were almost black, this man had bright green eyes and lighter skin and hair. In fact, his short-cropped hair was almost blond it was so light brown. It looked like a natural color, too.

"It's in the works though," he continued. "Courtesy of moi." He jabbed a thumb toward his chest. Leaning forward, he looked at the book in her hand. "That one isn't bad. Until mine comes out of course." He wagged his eyebrows at her.

"I'll keep an eye out for it."

He leaned on the counter, chewing casually on a straw. "You can hear all about it if you come to our Ghost, Voodoo, and Cemetery tour. Eight p.m. right here." He hit the counter with his open palm. "We even stop at some cool bars you might not see otherwise," he added, shifting toward her and lowering his voice, like he was sharing a secret.

"Sounds good. I'll see what my friends want..." Her words trailed off as the faint chime of the door along with the corresponding, overwhelming creak of old hinges in need of an oiling momentarily drew her attention.

Out of the corner of her eye she caught sight of the giggling couple leaving. On the sidewalk outside stood a woman in early 19th century clothing. She recognized the long camel-colored wool coat with a hint of low-heeled leather boots showing beneath and the tendrils of blond hair peeking from under her bonnet.

Unbelieving, she stared. It couldn't be.

She stepped forward to get a better look just as the couple obstructed her view. When they'd moved enough she could see past them, the woman was gone.

This couldn't be her imagination. She might believe the painting's eyes looking alive and sinister was all in her head, but seeing a woman in historical clothing...clothing identical to the ones in her dream? It was too much to ignore.

She had to figure out what was going on. She needed to figure it out. It was rooted deep inside her gut, so strong it was almost making her nauseous.

Without a word to either Xavier or the other man, she tossed the book on the counter and ran out of the shop, shoving past the couple still partially blocking the door.

"That was weird," Julien noted as the door slammed behind the blonde.

"When doesn't something weird happen in this city?" Xavier said dismissively.

Although honestly, he wasn't sure what to think. He'd watched her turn toward the door when it opened, watched her smile drop, watched the shock cross her pretty face, watched her stare at an empty spot on the sidewalk. She'd run out of the shop chasing *something*, he was sure of it. But what, he couldn't begin to guess.

It was more than that, though. She seemed so familiar to him. Her face, her mannerisms, her smile... He couldn't quite pinpoint where he'd seen her. Or if he ever even had.

So that coupled with her quick escape... Weird only began to describe it.

"Maybe she saw a friend," he told his brother as he returned the book to the bookshelf.

She definitely saw *something*, but it wasn't a friend. More like a ghost.

"Maybe she decided she really had to take a piss."

Typical crude Julien...

"Sure," Xavier said dryly. "Well, thanks for being twenty minutes late. You're lucky I live here and can open the store."

Julien's grin was lopsided. "Anytime."

Xavier headed for the back room. "I'll be sure to repay the favor tonight."

"No you won't," Julien said behind him. "Your head would explode if you were late."

Glad to finally be away from the store and away from the endless parade of tourists, Xavier crossed the back altar-room and ducked into the downstairs kitchen.

"Good afternoon, Xavier."

His grandmother didn't shift her clouded gaze to

him when he entered the room. Her unseeing eyes remained unfocused on nothing in particular as she added oils and other liquids to a large bowl, giving each bottle a quick sniff before adding the contents. He was always amazed how much she could do without sight.

He kissed her cheek. "Afternoon, Grandmere. Are you hungry? Have you had lunch yet?"

"I ate."

"Well, I'm getting ready to take off, do you need anything first?"

She opened a bottle, the smell of peppermint so strong it was unmistakable. Two dashes splashed into the bowl. "Every day you ask me and every day I tell you no."

"I know."

She was so independent she was stubborn. But he couldn't help checking up on her. She was seventy, blind, and diabetic. Someone needed to make sure she was well and had everything she needed. That someone certainly wouldn't be Julien or their mother.

"Someday you will though."

"Shut your mouth, boy. You'll curse me with your words."

He shook his head fondly. "Well, call me if you need me."

Vigorously stirring the ingredients in her bowl, she waved him off. As he turned to leave, she began to sing, her aged voice wavering slightly but still strong and beautiful.

She always sang. Whenever there was a quiet moment, sometimes when there wasn't. He always found it soothing, comforting. Probably because she'd been singing to him since he was a baby.

The old dining room was filled with flickering

candles when he stepped into it, which only meant one thing...

"Hey. Hey. Hey!" His mother frantically rushed over and pushed repeatedly on his chest. She wasn't pushing particularly hard—not that it would matter if she did since he outweighed her by at least eighty pounds—but he still let her move him backward. "You can't be here. I have a client coming."

"I just need to get upstairs." He pointed to the stairwell across the room.

She pushed him back again. "Oh no. My client wants complete privacy. You'll have to use the back stairs."

"Mother, there's no one here. It'll take me two seconds to cross the room."

"Huh-uh. No way. Just go around." She gave him one more shove for emphasis before turning away. Muttering, she started searching the floor of the room, flipping up the cloth on the circular table at the center to look underneath, and turning over the decorative pillows lined against the wall. "I know it's here somewhere," she said.

He was tempted to dash across the room anyway, but she'd probably have a nervous breakdown if he did. The woman wasn't exactly stable. Actually, she was a complete flake. She could barely take care of herself or handle day-to-day responsibilities. It was no wonder his dad took off when he was eight.

Her muttering had become more urgent and pillows were now being tossed around the room.

"Do you need my help?" he asked.

"God, are you still here? You gotta go! Now!"

He held up his hands in surrender. "No worries. I've already left." The French doors closed behind him with a heavy *thunk*.

Heading for the store, he had to cross back through the room reserved for his grandmother's rituals and blessings and whatever else she did in there. A flash of light caught on the altar and he paused. It couldn't have come from his mother's candles; the closed doors were solid wood. Only a beaded curtain separated this room from the store, so maybe it came from there. Maybe...

He rarely paid the altars much attention. Since the altar of Sanite Villere was in the shop, he was forced to talk about it on a daily basis. This one though... He passed it a million times and barely looked at it, though he did like to toss trinkets into its offering basket from time-to-time.

The altar was for Laurent Villere, his great (times ten) grandfather. According to Grandmere, Laurent was an influential Houngan in his day. A successful businessman, he ran an apothecary shop out of this very house. Both he and his sister, Sanite, were the bastard children of Benoît Villere, a wealthy Frenchman in the business of importing fine goods from the West Indies, including sugar and slaves. Not all that uncommon in the early days in New Orleans, Laurent had been educated in Paris, and great grandfather (times eleven), Benoît, had even left them and their mother, a mixed woman of Choctaw and African descent, an inheritance when he died.

Xavier had heard the stories over and over as a kid. But he'd never really thought about the man behind them. He wasn't sure why he did now.

Pulling a few coins from his pocket, he placed them into the small basket below Laurent's portrait. "Hope that pleases you, Grandpere," he said with a smile. He didn't believe for a second that offering gifts to the spirits of dead ancestors strengthened them, but it was worth a chuckle. Grandmere, his mother, and he was pretty sure Julien, definitely believed it.

The image of a woman, running toward him with a beaming smile on her beautiful face, flashed in his mind. Tumbling emotions washed over him—a mixture of elation, love, and sadness.

He recognized the brief flash from a recurring dream he occasionally had. Why he thought of it now, he had no idea. Shaking it off, he pushed through the beaded curtains and into the store.

Lottie followed after the blond woman for several blocks. She was always just out of reach. Every time Lottie got closer, the woman would disappear from view, rounding the corner to another street. She would run full speed to keep from losing her, only to catch a glimpse of her back as she disappeared behind another building.

She felt like she was being pulled along. Not just by her curiosity, but by something external. Like a piece of fine silk thread was attached to her midsection and some master puppeteer was tugging it with just enough force she complied but not hard enough to break the thread.

It was hard to say how long she followed. The buildings and people and cars began to blur until all she saw was the sidewalk stretched out before her, and the woman. She was vaguely aware of sweat pooling on her forehead and dripping between her breasts, of her lungs rapidly expanding and contracting, of the muscles in her legs beginning to burn. All she could think about was following the woman. She had to get somewhere. She didn't know where, but she had to find it.

Abruptly, the sensation changed from pulling to pushing. Even more intense than before, she couldn't ignore it as it shoved her feet forward. A voice inside her mind screeched at her to stop, but the destination was just ahead, just within reach, and all she could do was focus on the goal of getting there.

The blaring honk of a car horn followed by the rush of air as the quickly moving vehicle sped by, snapped her out of the trance. Startled, Lottie looked around and realized she was standing in the middle of a lane on an incredibly busy street.

A horn of another car, this time a large delivery truck, made her scramble back to the curb where she crumpled to her knees and clutched her chest like her hand might keep her heart from bursting through the bone.

She'd walked right into traffic! She could have been killed! She hadn't even seen the cars or registered the street. She'd been so focused on finding what could have easily been a figment of her imagination, she'd tuned out everything around her. It was like she'd been possessed.

The shrill ring of her phone brought her even further back into reality.

"Where the hell are you?" Amanda chirped through the headpiece. "I've sent you, like, five texts."

"Um..." Pushing to her feet, Lottie glanced down at her phone. Sure enough, there were five texts. She certainly hadn't heard the alerts. Glancing up and down the street, she didn't see a glimmer of the blond woman.

She took a breath to try and clear her head. "Heading back from the Voodoo shop," she lied. "What's up?"

"Just making sure you didn't get lost." She could tell by Amanda's tone she was joking and on her way to being completely inebriated. "And to see if you wouldn't mind picking up some beer or something on the way back. Drinks are a little spendy at the hotel bar."

"Sure." Would they notice if she brought non-alcoholic beer? Probably.

"Awesome! See you in a few!"

When the phone went dead and she moved to head back to the hotel, she suddenly realized she had no idea where she was. In fact, she had to pull up a map on her phone to figure it out.

God, what the hell was going on with her? The entire morning was this confusing, numb blur. Like she was still drunk and only remembering patchy details that didn't make any sense. Hell, maybe she *was* still drunk.

If she hadn't felt sober before, being nearly smooshed by a five-ton truck had a way of sobering up a girl. She was pretty sure she could recite the alphabet backwards while touching her nose while hopping on one foot down a straight line.

The only part of her morning that had made sense, that she might like to repeat, was meeting Xavier, the proprietor of the Voodoo shop. Maybe she should head back there...

And do what exactly?

She could pick up that book...

And then what? How did she explain running out of the shop?

Maybe it was best to simply go back to the hotel, meet up with Amanda and Sam, lounge in the pool. Maybe later they could hit up the tour...

She took another deep breath. That's exactly what

24

she'd do. Hopefully, it would give her enough time to come back to earth.

CHAPTER THREE

Wading in one corner of the pool, Sam was busily chatting up a couple of tan, freshly waxed guys. The twirl of her finger in her hair and the way she sipped the last little bit of her red frozen drink while keeping her focus firmly on guy number one as he spouted an animated story told Lottie that Sam probably wouldn't be staying in their room tonight.

With what looked like fresh drinks in hand, Amanda squeezed into the mix, sitting on the pool edge and dangling her feet into the water. She handed off one of the drinks—another frozen concoction—to Sam and then proceeded to drink the top third of her cocktail in one long slurp.

Standing across the pool from the foursome, six-pack of beer in hand, Lottie contemplated what to do. She wasn't sure she wanted to join what could easily turn into a make-out fest at any moment. The scene was all too familiar: Amanda and Sam drinking way too much and shacking up with the first cute guys they meet. Always the mom, it had Lottie worried. They didn't know these guys from Adam, but by the look of things, it wouldn't be long before Amanda and Sam would be getting to know them in the biblical sense.

Afraid this would happen, she had been skeptical about joining them on this trip and now it seemed the skepticism was justified.

Maybe if she slowly walked backward without making any sudden movements she could leave without being seen.

Not a chance.

"Lottie! Awesome, you're here!" Amanda enthusiastically waved her over.

She masked her grimace with a broad smile. Holding up the beer, she crossed the courtyard. "Hope you like Abita."

"If it's beer I like it!" guy number two exclaimed with a laugh. It was all she could do to keep from rolling her eyes.

She handed the beer to Amanda's outstretched hand. She set it down and the men immediately went for bottles.

"Thanks for picking this up," guy number one said.

"No problem."

"Hey, put your suit on and join us."

"Yeah," Sam chimed in. "Let's get this party started!"

From what Lottie saw, it already was.

Ignoring the little nagging voice in her head that warned of alcohol poisoning and chastised her for day drinking, she ducked into their suite and quickly slipped on her swimsuit.

She knew why she hesitated joining the others, why she was so wary of drinking too much, or losing control. After all, she'd watched her foster siblings struggle with drug and alcohol dependence, and she understood why it was such an easy vice for them, and her, to fall into. One drink to numb the pain. Two drinks to feel less alone. Three drinks to fit in with the crowd. Four drinks to disappear into another reality. She could easily follow that path. She nearly had.

But she also knew her wariness was keeping her an outsider. That judging her peers for being normal twenty-two-year-olds kept her alone. She remembered that when she took a beer from guy number one and sat next to Amanda on the pool edge.

Introductions were made and Lottie learned that Rick (guy number one) and Steve (guy number two) were from San Diego State University. It was fitting given their surfer good looks. They were nothing but nice to her and even though the conversation was interlaced with plenty of high-fives and drunken battle calls, she had to admit her initial assessment of them was harsh. Her initial assessment of a lot of people was harsh.

She tried to push everything out of her brain—the weird dreams, the weird portrait at the Voodoo shop, and the really weird part where she nearly killed herself rushing into traffic—and focus on being a normal college student on spring break in New Orleans.

Before registering it, she'd quickly downed the beer in her hand. Amanda cheered when she set the empty bottle aside. And when she grabbed another beer from the now two-pack, even Sam smiled. It was so strange how they placed so much emphasis on everyone being at a similar level of drunkenness. No one wanted to be the drunkest person there, she supposed. She *was* feeling less uptight and relaxed already. Slippery slope indeed.

"That's what I'm talking about!" Sam said to her before tuning to the rest of the group. "You guys want shots?"

A few hours later her head was swimming in a fuzzy sea. Sam was making out with Rick, her back pressed against the pool wall, legs wrapped around his waist. From the close way they were talking, it wouldn't be long before Amanda and Steve followed suit.

Lottie stumbled to their room to pee and probably, possibly, definitely, lie down for a little bit. A full afternoon of sun and a few too many cocktails and she was zapped. She had a fleeting thought of giving up the back bedroom so Amanda and Sam could shack up in there if they wanted, but the promise of a soft bed out of the heat and afternoon sun quickly pushed it away. Besides the bedroom, there was also a loft and a couch in the hotel suite. She was pretty sure they'd manage.

After emptying her bladder she decided to refill it with a huge glass of water. And then another. The cool liquid felt so good sliding down her throat, she splashed some on her face and then through her hair. And *that* water felt so good on her chlorine-coated skin, she decided a shower was in order. It was like she had a layer of pool crust on her skin. Not something she wanted to share with the sheets.

The water started out cool, but once the temperature of her skin dropped a few degrees she was actually cold and turned up the heat until steam rolled through the room. She made a half-ass attempt to lather up and mush some conditioner through her hair but mostly she just leaned against the shower wall and let the water help sober her up.

"Charlotte," a whisper, a trickle, murmured. Barely audible, she ignored it.

"Charlotte."

Her eyes cracked open as the sound merged with the spray of her shower. That was definitely her name but she couldn't tell where it was coming from. It seemed to be a part of the falling water itself. She still wasn't sure she'd actually heard anything but falling water.

"Charlotte."

The words were louder this time. They seemed to start at the showerhead and end at the tub drain. She perked up her ears, listening for sounds of someone moving about in the room. There was nothing—only the patter of water on porcelain.

"Charlotte."

She definitely heard that. A woman's voice. It still sounded like it was coming from the water.

"Amanda? Sam?" she called into the room, pushing off the wall. "Are you guys out there?"

No one answered.

Maybe she really was imagining it. Like when you're worried about missing your alarm clock and being late for something important and in your half-awake state you keep hearing the alarm go off even though there's an hour before you have to get up. This was like that.

"Charlotte." The words were said right into her ear, as clear as day, as though someone was standing next to her.

She screamed and spun around. There was nothing there.

She slammed the shower off—just in case the voice actually *was* coming from the water.

Liquid dripping from her body, heart racing, she stood frozen in place, too scared to move. Straining, she listened for the voice. All she heard was the roaring of air as it heaved in and out of her lungs.

The welcome silence was broken by the even more welcome sound of Amanda, Sam, Rick, and Steve crashing into the room. Laughter followed the sound of something falling on the floor.

She was finally able to move. She was going crazy. That's all there was to it.

After toweling off, she slipped into a tank and shorts and joined the others.

"Lottie!" Amanda slurred, holding up a fresh Daiquiri.

She sat on the arm of the sofa. "What's up?"

"Where have you been? We were looking everywhere for you." The glassiness to Amanda's eyes told her it didn't matter what she said, the words would fall on uncomprehending ears.

"Just taking a shower," she said anyway. "Hey, I'm going to crash in the back room. Is that okay with you?"

Sam and Rick had already disappeared into the loft and Amanda just stared at her as she swayed unsteadily on her feet.

Lottie rose. "Okay, cool." She wasn't keen on being alone but she had a feeling things were going to get naked quick and she'd rather not be there when they did.

"Hey." Steve grabbed her arms as she turned to leave. "Why don't you join us?"

She gently pulled her arm from his grasp. "Naw. I'm beat. You guys have fun though." To avoid being grabbed again, she darted into the back bedroom, locking the door behind her.

Once alone in the room she began to feel uneasy. Like an eight-year-old, she checked under the bed first, then the closet, and finally the bathroom. Just like before the room was empty. In her drunken state, she must have imagined it.

And the woman on the street? And the staring eyes in the painting? And the über realistic dream?

Lottie sat on the bed and drew her knees to her chest. What was happening to her? And why? It didn't make sense.

Maybe she'd been drugged. Maybe someone slipped her something last night and the effects hadn't worn off yet. It had to be something like that. Nothing else made sense.

Or she was so tired she was hallucinating. She'd only gotten maybe four hours of sleep the night before.

The sounds of sex drifted in from the other room just as a huge yawn stretched her jaws wide. A nap was exactly what she needed, not only to sober her up, but also to erase the fatigue coursing through her bones. Thankfully, she had earplugs.

"Rosette!" Élise called as she stepped into the mudroom, carefully shedding her coat and the water collected on it. "I have the calomel. How is Amélie?"

The servant hustled into the room, quickly taking her coat and bonnet. "She's sleeping now, Madame, but," Rosette looked over her shoulder, "you have a caller."

"Now?" Élise glanced around the small woman's frame. All she could make out was the kitchen and a corner of the sitting room. "Who is it?"

Of all the times to receive a caller... The bottom three inches of her dress was soaked, her boots tracked wet footprints, and she hated to imagine what her hair looked like. With all the humidity, probably a mess of unruly curls.

"The American."

"Henry?" The question was mostly rhetorical. She only knew one American who would be calling on her, especially in this weather. Not that she knew that many Americans. Few mingled with French Creole society and most seemed to look upon her culture with disdain, something she could not understand.

Rosette nodded, a grin spreading on her round face. "Second time this week. I believe he's taken with you."

"Perhaps." Élise hadn't decided whether that was good news or not. As a widow—even one with a degree of financial security—without a means of support, her position was still somewhat precarious. Henry seemed to have a pleasant demeanor and he was certainly wealthy enough to offer her and her children all the security they could ever want. But not only did she not feel that way for him, he was a Protestant.

She might be able to overlook their religious differences if she could find a hint of love for him in her heart, but she couldn't. Not yet. And though she felt selfish for admitting it, she rather liked the freedom she currently enjoyed.

Still, she wasn't ready to dismiss his affection just yet, and she couldn't be rude by turning him away, so she made an attempt to smooth her hair and her dress with the palms of her hands and with a smile to Rosette, joined him in the sitting room.

"Henry," she greeted warmly, trying her best to use the English pronunciation.

Standing by the fire, he immediately turned to greet her, stopping feet from where she stood. She curtseyed and he bowed.

"What do I...owe...the...pleasure of your...visit?" *Her English was halting to say the least, and she spoke very little of it. Most Creoles she knew wouldn't even attempt to learn the language, but she knew it would someday be necessary. More and more Americans were coming to the city every day. This arrangement wasn't temporary as her people hoped. The Americans were here to stay.*

"I came to personally invite you to a dinner. At my home," *Henry replied in French. His French was much better than her English and she was grateful he chose to speak it. English was such a rough language on her tongue.* "At my new home," *he continued, holding out a sealed envelope.*

"Merci," *she said, taking the envelope. It was lovely paper, the grain so fine she could barely see it and bleached to a bright white with Henry's family seal prominently displayed in the red wax.* "So your new home is finished?" *The Americans, at least the wealthy ones, were building beautiful, large homes up river, including a massive Protestant church on the riverside corner of Canal and Bourbon.*

"It is. The furnishings were delivered yesterday."

His smile revealed teeth that were beginning to yellow from too much tobacco. It really didn't detract much from his rugged, sun-worn good looks. But the way it made Élise cringe at the thought of his mouth anywhere near hers in an intimate way was a bold reminder she had no desire for him in her heart.

"I would very much love for you to join me," *he continued.*

She glanced at the paper in her hands and then at Henry, and smiled. "Of course. I would be honored."

"Mama!" *Amélie's small voice wailed down the stairs from the bedrooms above.*

Rosette stepped forward. "I'll get her."

"Mama!" Amélie cried again, her tiny voice filled with anguish and tears.

It ripped through Élise's heart. She held out her arm to stop Rosette. "No, no. I should go." She turned to Henry. "I'm sorry, but I—"

He gestured toward the stairs. "Tend to your child."

She hustled for the stairway, pausing just as she stepped onto the bottom step. "Thank you for calling," she said and then hurried up the steps.

CHAPTER FOUR

Xavier was so used to dismissing the door chime with a simple, "Welcome to Villere House of Voodoo", that he didn't bother looking up from his computer until Julien's voice sounded in his ear.

"Well, look who's back. I never expected to see her again."

It was the blonde from earlier that day. The one who'd run out like she'd seen the ghost of Hitler. He rarely agreed with anything his brother said, thought, or did, but this was one time when he shared Julien's sentiment. She *was* the last person he expected to see again. Ever. He couldn't say he was disappointed.

The expression on her face was both wary and excited. And curious. She took in the store like she was looking for clues. She'd done that earlier too, only then she'd been more curious and confused. The fear wasn't there either.

It was definitely intriguing.

"Oh. Looks like she brought an entourage this time."

Sure enough, two girls followed closely behind her. One blond like she was, only an unnatural shade, the other with sleek brown hair that looked plastic.

"Now that's a trio I'd love to dogpile."

Xavier gave his brother a *look*. Yes, they were all attractive women, but *dogpile*? "Can you get any sleazier?"

"Coming from the guy who bangs a different girl every week..." Julien rolled his eyes. "You're such a crit."

"Hardly every week." But close. He couldn't deny that lately he'd been with more different women than he'd admit out loud. Unlike Julien, he wasn't about sticking his cock in every piece of tail he could. It just seemed to work that way. But also unlike Julien, he wasn't exactly proud of it.

The runaway girl from earlier that day approached them. "Is it too late to sign up for the tour?"

"Not at all," Julien shoved off the counter. "Xavier can hook you up." He sized her up as he walked past before tossing an arm around each of her friends. "So, ladies, ready to have your mind blown?"

"It's good to see you," Xavier said when they joined the rest of the tour group waiting on the sidewalk. "I honestly wasn't expecting to. You really bolted out of here earlier."

"Sorry. I just..." The furrow grew deep between her brows as she trailed off. "You know, I would really like that book. You still have it?"

He was so swept up studying the myriad of emotions crossing her pretty face the question caught him off guard. "Yeah. Yeah, of course. I put it away but it should be right..." He pointed to the bookshelf as he stepped from behind the cash register to help her.

"Oh! I see it." They reached for the book at the

same time and his hand brushed hers before he was able to pull back, like accidentally touching someone was taboo or something.

The way his body reacted though, maybe there was some justification in the *taboo*. He just wanted to touch her more, like a lot more.

Guilty heat flashed in her eyes when she looked at him. Did that mean she felt it too?

Whatever she felt, she covered it up with a smile that looked just a hair too big. "Can't wait to read it," she said, holding up the book.

"Yeah, probably a good one for the plane."

"I'm here for a few more days, so I plan on knocking this one out."

For some reason that made him happy. "You'll have to tell me how you like it."

Her smile widened, making her look positively radiant. "I will."

Like an idiot, he just stood there for a while, staring at her.

"Lottie! You get the tickets yet?" It was one of her friends, the one with the plastic looking hair.

"Just getting ready to," *Lottie* said, turning to him expectantly.

"Of course." He returned behind the counter and rang her up. "Lottie…that's an interesting name. Is it short for something?"

"Charlotte. I'm not sure if I like it or not. Kind of reminds me of Lassie."

He laughed. "Well, then I'll be sure to call you Charlotte."

"Oh, you can call me Lottie. Everyone does. Just don't whistle when you do it." She handed over the cash.

"Wouldn't dream of it," he said as he made

change. "Hey, have a good time. Don't let Julien scare you. He likes to do that in the cemetery."

Her smile dropped and she nodded tensely. "Thanks," she clipped before turning and heading out of the store.

Another weird response. But instead of just writing it off like he normally would, it intrigued him. *She* intrigued him. That didn't happen often.

Lottie had a hard time paying attention to their tour guide, a man she learned was Julien Villere. Obviously related to Xavier, though she couldn't be sure how. There was *some* similarity to their facial structure but the green eyes, light brown hair, and lighter skin tone made it hard to believe they were even cousins.

The snippets of the tour she heard sounded interesting enough. Unfortunately, she was too much inside her own head to take much of it in. She kept replaying her latest dream. It had been even more real, more clear. Like she'd actually been there.

Maybe it was some alcohol fueled delusion, but didn't feel like it. But it was too weird to imagine anything else. She had been intoxicated both times she'd dreamt of Élise Cantrelle. *Could* she be remembering a book she'd read long ago and forgotten? A movie? It didn't seem likely, plus how did that explain Sanite Villere? Or the shower, or the strange woman on the street, or the road incident…

The craziness of it was making her head hurt. It certainly made paying attention to the tour impossible.

It wasn't until they approached a busy roadway and the scenery became shockingly familiar that her attention finally snapped back to the present. This was it. This was where she'd nearly walked—no, where she'd nearly been *pushed* into traffic.

And as the group crossed the street, she finally realized where they were headed—the cemetery.

Okay, now her head was officially fucked. Once again she felt like she was in a trance, only this one was her own doing. She could only stare, only numbly follow as Julien guided them through the dark, crumbling cemetery.

After a brief introduction of the history and why's of the above-ground cemetery, they traveled haphazardly through the raised tombs, weaving through narrow walkways that were maze-like in their seemingly unplanned paths.

Midway down an aisle that looked identical to the aisle before, Lottie felt the gentle tug that was becoming frighteningly all too familiar. The same pull that led her to the Villere House of Voodoo. The same pull that tried to lead her here.

She ignored it. Or tried to.

The more she resisted the more insistent the pull became until it settled in her stomach in a pool of nausea. She swallowed against the bile and made one last attempt to resist the urge to follow when fog settled over her vision and seeped into her brain.

She was barely aware of what happened next. She felt herself stop and walk away from the group, toward one of tombs. Felt herself reach into her purse and retrieve something smooth and hard.

The next moments were even blurrier. Pain seared her palm, trailing to her wrist. Her hand stretched forward. Cries of alarm sounded and she was yanked backward. There was a face directly in front of hers, but it was a screaming smear of indistinguishable features and noises. Then her body began to violently shake.

And like that, the fog lifted.

Amanda stood before her, a hand on each of her shoulders, face inches from hers as she screamed, "Lottie! Lottie! Wake the fuck up!" over and over again while shaking her back and forth.

"Okay," she said, her voice too quiet as it slid from her mouth.

Amanda was still shaking her. Other people from the tour filtered over and now formed a curious mob.

Searching her throat and finding her voice, Lottie yelled, "Okay! Enough!"

Finally, Amanda released her.

Julien pushed his way through the crowd. "What the hell...?" he gasped.

Still feeling dazed, stunned, and very much confused, she took in her surroundings. In her right hand, she held her nail file like a weapon, the *blade* tinged with red. Her left hand throbbed and she glanced down at it. Blood dripped from an angry looking slash that extended from her wrist across her palm.

She quickly closed her hand and slipped the file back into her purse, but not before Sam exclaimed, "Oh my God, Lottie! What are you trying to do, kill yourself or something?"

"Of course not. It just slipped..." she drifted off as her attention was drawn away from her friend and toward the tomb closest too her. She approached the grave. Was this what she'd been reaching for?

The engraving was worn, but the name was clear:
Élise Cantrelle
1788-1816

"It can't be..."

A strong arm wrapped around her shoulders and pulled her away from the grave. She didn't resist but stared up at Julien in surprise.

"Don't worry everyone, she is fine. Possessed by a Loa, compelled by the spirit to visit her ancestor's grave." He turned to Lottie. "You've been neglectful to your great-great-great-grandmother's memory haven't you?" He winked.

She couldn't do anything but smile feebly. The gathered crowd gave a little uneasy chuckle.

"Unfortunately, she accidentally cut her hand on the fence. You should probably go to the hospital," he said to her. "Get that taken care of."

She nodded and he released her shoulders. "So," he said to the crowd. "Who's ready to see the grave of the infamous Voodoo Queen, Marie Laveau?"

The crowd began shuffling away. Amanda joined Lottie but Sam moved with the group. "Sam!" Amanda called.

With an obvious sigh, Sam turned around. "What?"

Amanda stared at her. "We're going to the hospital."

"I don't think we all need to go. It's not like she's dying."

"You're fucking kidding me—"

"No. It's cool." Lottie smiled. "Go ahead, Sam. I'll catch up with you later." She turned to Amanda. "You can go too. I'll grab a cab."

"I'm not leaving you alone."

"Thanks, but—"

"Seriously Lottie. What the hell happened? One minute you're fine and the next you're all zombified and stabbing yourself."

"I have no idea. Really. I've been out of it all day.

I feel like someone slipped me some drugs."

That option didn't seem too farfetched to Amanda as she considered it. "Well, I wish they'd share."

"No, you don't. This hasn't been fun, trust me."

Amanda glanced at her hand, still clenched into a fist and still dripping blood. "I guess not. C'mon, let's get that shit taken care of so we can get back to the party. You owe me a couple drinks for this," she added with a grin.

The ER doctor, a Dr. Anderson, did not seemed convinced by Lottie's fabricated story. He looked at the wound, looked at her, and then looked at the wound again. "Fence, huh?"

"Yeah. I was holding onto one of the spikes on the top and slipped." It sounded plausible enough.

"Hmm." It was said with the tone every adult used when they knew someone was lying but didn't feel like arguing. "Well, you'll need a few more stitches." He turned to Amanda, absorbed by something on her phone. "And no more fences," he said to her.

Her head jerked up and she pressed her hand with the phone cupped inside to her lap, like she was hiding the screen. She was probably just watching a funny video or reading some celebrity gossip article, but she gave them a guilty, sheepish smile. "Of course. No fences."

Dr. Anderson turned back to Lottie. His eyes looked weary, like he was lacking a few hours of sleep. Or maybe a week's worth. "No more fences."

She shook her head earnestly and then offered what she hoped was a convincing smile. She hadn't tried to kill herself (as far as she knew) and she really hoped he believed her. Last thing she wanted was for this middle-aged man, who seemed nice enough, to commit her because he thought she might be a danger to herself or others.

"Just beer and beads for me from now on."

His gaze lingered on hers for a few moments before he nodded. "Okay," he said. "Let's get you stitched up."

Thirty minutes and fifteen stitches later and they were back on the streets heading toward the French Quarter.

CHAPTER FIVE

When Amanda wanted to stop at the hotel room to pee before meeting up with Sam, Lottie knew it was the perfect opportunity for her to bail on the evening.

"You're kidding me? You want to stay in?"

"I'm exhausted. And my hand kinda hurts."

"Alcohol will take care of that."

"And the exhausted part?"

"Caffeine," Amanda said with a shrug. "Oh, wait. I think I have a couple Adderalls in my purse."

She started to dig through the bright red bag when Lottie's look stopped her.

"Right. You sure you don't want one? Just this one time? Adderall is harmless. Shit, they prescribe it to kids."

"I think sleep would probably be better for me. I'll party tomorrow night I promise. But I just can't tonight. I don't have it in me."

Amanda sighed. "All right." She held out her hand. "Give me your nail file."

"What?"

"I know you said you weren't trying to hurt yourself, but still, I'd feel better if you weren't armed.

45

Just in case you go all wacko again or something."

Though the request was somewhat shocking, it certainly wasn't unreasonable. "Sure." She handed it over.

The file went into Amanda's purse and her arms went around Lottie's neck. Amanda was a confirmed hugger but Lottie never minded the sometimes awkward displays of affection. Especially not now.

"Hey, thanks for everything, Amanda. And if you and Sam need a designated *walker*, call me. You know, like if you get lost…" She grinned.

"Will do." Amanda started for the door. "And if you change your mind and want to hang, text me."

She wasn't sure what could possibly make her want to brave the dirt and grime of Bourbon Street, but agreed anyway.

Once alone, the room seemed eerily quiet. She turned on the TV and then every light in the suite. Plopping on the couch, she tried to push the day's events from her mind. If she thought about them, even for a second, she was afraid she might lose her mind.

It was an impossible task. Nothing on the television was working. She sifted through boring show after show, finally settling on the pre-recorded live cable feed from New Orleans Historical Homes City Council. One woman's plea to keep her not quite historically accurate shutters kept Lottie's attention for a few minutes. It wasn't enough.

She was invariably brought back to the incident on the street, or the shower *talking* to her, or the weirdest point of the day where, in some sort of daze, she'd sliced her wrist in the cemetery. Then to top it off, she kept going back to her dreams. Élise, Rosette, Henry, Amélie, Sanite Villere… It made her want to slam her head into the wall until there was nothing but pudding inside.

There was really only one shining spotlight on the day. One thing that made her head spin in an entirely different direction: Xavier Villere.

Meeting him was the one highlight of her day that was welcome, that felt good, that…she wanted to do again. Maybe she should be frightened of the spark she felt with him, but unlike the rest of the hoopla she was dealing with, at least being attracted to a man who happened to be gorgeous felt normal…real…natural. Dreaming about an early nineteenth century woman did not.

In spite of wondering whether the Historical Homes City Council would approve the current resident's desire to keep his recently installed vinyl windows, Lottie clicked off the TV with a sigh.

She needed to get to bed. She was just a little afraid of what was waiting for her when she closed her eyes. Would she dream again of Élise? Of Amélie? Would she hear strange voices again? Would she be compelled to hurt herself—maybe throw herself off the bed…into the pool…stuff her head into the oven…?

On cue her bandaged palm and wrist throbbed.

She groaned out loud and she hefted herself off the sunken couch and headed for the back bedroom.

Maybe it was all just alcohol withdrawal fueled delusions, but she left the lights on in the common room anyway. Just in case. Of course, Amanda and Sam would probably be pretty intoxicated when they stumbled through the door later, so she could mentally justify leaving the lights on for their benefit.

Knowing she'd never sleep with the bedroom light blazing, she clicked it off and then leapt from the door to the bed and under the covers in a single,

47

Olympics worthy bound. At least the open doorway provided allowed enough light to seep in it wasn't pitch-black.

In spite of her racing heart and throbbing arm, it wasn't long before her exhausted thoughts drifted into blackness.

"Mama!" Amélie called just as Élise reached the door to her room.

"I'm here, darling."

Amélie's room was dark and cool, but even in the dim light of a single lamp, Élise could see that she glistened with sweat.

"Il fait chaud, mama," Amélie whimpered, twisting in her soaked nightgown.

Élise sat on the edge of the small, feather stuffed mattress. After peeling back strands of Amélie's fine blond hair from her forehead, she placed the back of her hand against the child's skin. "Oh, mon petit chou, you are warm." Amélie hadn't had the fever when she left to retrieve the calomel. It was alarming that it could appear so quickly. "Rosette," she called toward the open door.

Within minutes the petite servant was standing in the doorway. Backlit from the brighter light in the hall, all Élise could make out was the white of her apron. "Please bring in some cool water and a fresh cloth."

"Yes, Madame."

"And the medicine," Élise added as Rosette turned to leave.

They spent the night alternating between trying to soothe Amélie's fever and holding her over the bourdalou as the calomel caused her to retch nearly every hour. Getting her to take the medicine took both of them—Élise held her arms while Rosette forced the liquid into her. Even though it was mixed with sugar water, Amélie still resisted, screaming and twisting in Élise's grasp.

She hated it all. Couldn't stand watching her youngest child so miserable.

After hours of retching and still no reduction in fever, she was beginning to question giving Amélie the medicine at all. Especially after what the stranger on the street had said. The doctor assured her it was necessary, but it didn't seem to be helping. In fact, the child only seemed worse, finally collapsing from exhaustion sometime after midnight. Élise quickly followed.

By morning the fever had deepened. She refused to give her daughter any more of the calomel, sending Rosette for the doctor instead. The boys were thankfully at school, so they didn't have to see her cry.

She waited all morning, desperately applying as much cool water to Amélie's forehead as she could. By the time the doctor arrived, shortly after noon, her nerves were so frazzled it was all she could do to keep from snapping at him for being so late. Nor did she care that her hair was loose and she still wore her dressing gown.

He sat in the chair Élise had vacated upon his arrival to examine Amélie's pale, listless body. After a few moments he turned to Élise. "You gave her the calomel?"

"Yes. She was sick all night."

"Hmm." He leaned back in the chair and stroked the short gray hairs on his chin. "You'll need to take her to the Barber. A pint should be enough to remove

the tainted blood."

"I can't take her anywhere. Look at her!" She pointed at her daughter. The doctor barely turned. "Isn't there anything you can do now...?"

He grimaced.

"Please," she begged. "She must get better."

"Children often don't recover, Madame Cantrelle. You know that."

Bracing against the dresser, Élise closed her eyes and tried to keep her breath and tears in check. He was right, she knew. She'd been lucky that all of her children had been healthy thus far. She lost one child to miscarriage, but that was it.

She couldn't lose Amélie. She'd finally gotten over Nathanael's unexpected death, to lose her little girl...

She swallowed. Hard. Hard enough the doctor probably heard it.

He sighed. "Very well. I'll do it." He sighed again, retrieving his bag from where it rested on the floor. "I'll need a pail and some clean water."

Scurrying from the room, she retrieved the items and with Rosette in tow, rushed back up the stairs.

Sleeves rolled up, the doctor had his tools on the chest and a pail at his feet. For a man so recently unwilling to perform the bloodletting, he certainly was prepared.

"I'll need your help with her." He gestured roughly toward the bed.

Sitting Amélie up, Élise held her shoulders while Rosette held her legs in case she struggled. It was unnecessary. Amélie barely flinched when he pierced her vein with the lancet, only moaning a little.

Élise had been bled several times in her life, most recently when she started having debilitating headaches. And it never bothered her. But watching the stream of red pour from her daughter's tiny, pale arm made her nauseous. And the more the pail filled, the sicker she felt until she finally had to turn away.

She squeezed Amélie gently, resting her cheek against the soft, blond hair. Kissing her head, she murmured, "All will be well. All will be well."

By evening, it was apparent neither the bleeding nor the calomel had helped. Fever continued to ravage Amélie's body, sweat soaking through three sleeping gowns and two sets of sheets. Élise refused to leave the room, not even when Rosette begged her to get some rest in a proper bed, promising the keep watch while she slept.

Finally, Rosette quit asking. The boys returned from school and she tended to them. Élise didn't know what she'd do without her. She was more like a sister than a servant. They'd been together since Nathanael's death. Presumably an ex-slave, Rosette had arrived in New Orleans with little more than the clothes on her back and desperately seeking work.

Seven months pregnant and trying to figure out how to simplify her household without a man to provide a steady income, Élise took an instant liking to the petite, wide-eyed woman.

The arrangement was perfect for both. Rosette provided almost all the assistance she needed, and maintaining one live-in servant was financially more feasible than an entire household.

The companionship she provided was priceless.

Élise smiled gratefully, if not a bit wearily, when Rosette brought a small baguette, some meat and cheese, and tea.

"You need to eat," she said, setting the plate on the dresser.

Even though her stomach turned at the sight of the food, she said, "Thank you. Are the boys in bed?"

"Yes. Washed and fed."

Élise sighed. "I should tell them goodnight, at least."

Rosette smiled reassuringly. "Don't worry Madame, they will be fine. They are strong young men." She stooped over Amélie, whose heavy breathing made her chest rise and fall like a set of billows. Gently, she rested her hand on the girl's glistening forehead, the dark skin looking even darker against Amélie's colorless complexion. Rosette kissed her forehead and then turned to Élise. "I am not so sure about this one's strength."

Élise felt her heart slide into her feet. "Don't say that," she whispered hoarsely, fighting the tears as they rushed to her eyes. She couldn't break down now. She needed to stay strong.

"I must say it." Rosette sat beside her and took her hand. "Just as I must say I know someone who might be able to help."

"The doctor—"

"Not a doctor," Rosette interjected. "Not a white one anyway."

Élise immediately knew she was speaking of a Voodoo healer.

"Before you think to refuse," Rosette said. "Know that I love this child as if she were my own. I helped deliver her. I've helped raise her. I wouldn't suggest the magic man unless I thought it would work."

She only had to look into Rosette's deep brown eyes for a moment to know the woman was sincere. It wasn't uncommon for French and Spanish Creoles to use the Voodoo healers for tonics and other various potions, but for something this serious...?

But Amélie was so weak and she was desperate. Rosette might be her servant but she was also a friend. A trusted friend.

Gently, she pulled her hand from Rosette's and turned to place a delicate kiss on Amélie's forehead. Her skin was so, so hot, the decision was instantly made. She turned to Rosette. "Send for your man. And please hurry."

The last sentence was unnecessary. Rosette was already hustling out the door.

Lottie felt like she'd barely slept at all even though the clock read two a.m. and she'd been asleep for four hours. She was as exhausted as the woman in her dreams. Both physically and mentally. Like she was the one who'd been up for hours with her sick daughter, watching her health continue to weaken.

What was even more baffling than the realism of the dreams and the fact that they were in French even though she'd never spoken a word of it, was the way they were being played out. Like someone had pushed play the moment she stepped foot in New Orleans, but it was a movie she could only watch while asleep. She had little doubt the next time she closed her eyes, the dream would pick up right where it had left off.

Kicking her feet over the side of the bed, she sat up and rubbed her eyes. The dreams weren't going to stop. She knew that now. They also weren't the result of too much alcohol because she'd gone to bed stone sober this time.

What did it all mean though? Was the ghost of Élise Cantrelle trying to tell her something? If so, why?

She felt crazy for even *thinking* she might be haunted.

Crazy she could justify. Being haunted was a little tougher to swallow. It could be some grand delusion. A story her subconscious was creating to distract her from her real fears: graduating college and entering the daunting world of the working adult without a supportive family. All alone. Always alone.

She'd had more than a few psychology classes and that scenario was much more feasible than the ghost scenario.

The lights were on in the other room but the suite was quiet, telling her Amanda and Sam were still out.

Remembering she hadn't brushed her teeth or washed her face, she padded to the bathroom. The moment she flipped on the faucet to wash her hands the energy in the room changed.

Or so her imagination declared. It was probably the memory of the shower incident making the hairs on the back of her neck stand up.

As she rinsed the toothpaste from her mouth, her name garbled from the stream of water. Faint at first and easy to ignore. But as she lathered up a wash cloth it grew stronger.

"Charlotte," it whispered. "Charlotte."

Every muscle in her body clenched tight. This had to be some weird malfunction of her brain. She rapidly scrubbed her face.

"Charlotte." Louder, clearer this time.

Rinsing the suds from her skin, she closed her eyes.

Think about something else. Think about something else.

"Écoutez!"

With a scream, she twisted the water off with so

much force her wrists hurt. Still clutching the knobs tight, she stood perfectly still. Listening. Panting. The only sound was the faint laughter of people partying in the courtyard. She listened for a good five minutes. Nothing. Absolutely nothing.

It was the shower all over again.

What was that last word? It was French, she knew that much. But she had no idea what it meant or if she'd even heard it correctly.

She stared at her image in the mirror. The woman greeting her was wide-eyed and shell-shocked, her hair a halo of messy blond curls. She barely recognized herself. She looked more like the woman in her dreams than the face she'd grown so accustomed to she barely saw it anymore.

Peeling her fingers from the faucet knobs, she slowly turned around, like any sudden move would bring the ghost back. Lottie swallowed. Hard.

Ghost… God, maybe she was going crazy.

She peered into the bedroom. The bedcover was a twisted, tousled heap, like someone had just finished a fantastic romp under the covers, but the room was otherwise undisturbed. And empty.

Tip-toeing through the bedroom, she approached the door to the sitting area with trepidation. Hand pressed against the jamb, heart thundering in her chest, she carefully inched forward until she could see into the room. The sofa pullout bed was still out, empty beer bottles and condom wrappers on the end table, but it too was empty.

It was a tense look around the second bathroom. Luckily the shower curtain was open so she wasn't subjected to the task of sliding it aside. Wasn't the shower where killers in movies often hid? Pulling back the curtain only revealed a masked man with a knife. Then the camera would pan to the bathroom mirror and blood would splatter across the glass.

She shuddered. Definitely a plus she was spared that.

The only place left where someone could be hiding was the upstairs loft.

Walking like she was trying to sneak out of the house while her parents slept, she crossed the room and climbed the stairs. Each step increased the pace of her heartbeat. By the time she reached the last step she felt like she'd just finished a marathon.

But there was nothing. Absolutely nothing.

In some ways she was relieved, but in other ways it just made the situation even freakier. Since it wasn't a flesh-and-bone person tormenting her, being alone didn't make her safe. If she couldn't see them, she couldn't hide from them.

She had to get out of there.

Even if she didn't feel like partying or entertaining drunk people on Bourbon, she had to find Sam and Amanda. She couldn't be alone. Not now.

Throwing on the first dress she pulled from her suitcase, she left her PJs on the floor. Her feet were barely in her sandals as she grabbed her purse and ran.

CHAPTER SIX

A few texts later, a phone call, and a quick look around at least ten different bars and Lottie still hadn't found her friends. Nor had she heard from them. She was about to give up, and do what she wasn't sure. They might be back at the room, but she wasn't ready to go there, not yet, not while she trembled every time she thought of the place.

Maybe she should belly up to a bar and enjoy a club soda. The drunk watching would probably provide a suitable distraction. As long as she stayed near people, she felt like she'd be safe.

Just as she'd decided on a place that seemed to have the right vibe—enough people but not too busy—her phone buzzed.

We're at Molly's on the Market, Amanda's text read. *Come out!*

Using her phone to map a course, she didn't waste any time heading that way.

She hadn't traveled long on the recommended route before the streets became quiet. The faint sounds of activity surrounded her, but the street she walked on was void of life.

Quickening her steps, she pushed forward and tried to not think about anything but putting one foot in front of the other. It worked for about five minutes. Nose to phone, she followed the path mapped out with only the occasional glance to verify the GPS location matched the street signs. It was a perfect system for getting somewhere quickly and *blindly* until she looked up and knew exactly where she was, despite the fact that she'd never actually been there.

The colors of some of the buildings had changed, the street looked different, but she still recognized all the buildings. Especially one.

She approached it with caution. The front shutters were drawn tight and painted a different color, but she knew it as much as she knew her childhood home.

This was the house from her dreams. The home Élise Cantrelle lived in. Lottie remembered entering in through the back room, soaked from a rainy walk home and dripping water.

Frozen in place, she wasn't sure what to do next. Her phone said she only had a couple blocks before arriving at *Molly's* and the safety of her friends, but she couldn't seem to move. This house... this was *the* house, Élise's house. How could she leave that?

She stood there for a few minutes, staring at the façade. Three stories with balconies on the second and third story. A narrow alley lead to a small courtyard. She could see it from where she stood, but more than that, she *remembered* it. And in the back, a larger courtyard separated the main house from the barn and servant's quarters. She wasn't sure how she knew that, since it hadn't been in her dreams, but she did. Just as she could picture so many details of the historic home. The layout of the stairs, the kitchen, Amélie's bedroom... What did it look like now? Were there apartments inside? Was it still a single-family home? And who lived there?

Chin tucked, posture hunched, hands shoved into pockets, a man approached the building from the opposite direction. Even though his face was hidden, Lottie knew exactly who he was. She'd spent an hour staring at him.

It was the doctor from the emergency room.

And he walked right into the alley like he owned the place. Hell, maybe he did.

Having something more familiar, more tangible than her odd dreams to tie her to the house gave her the confidence she needed to follow him. She hadn't thought of an excuse for why she was there when she reached the door, but it didn't stop her from knocking—she'd figure something out.

But the knocking got her nowhere. She knocked again. Music seeped through the closed door, but it wasn't the type of music one would expect a doctor to be playing at three a.m. It was hard, heavy, industrial dance music. The type played at bars…

She tested the knob and surprisingly it turned. The music didn't lie; pushing the door open did actually reveal a bar.

It should have made her feel more comfortable stepping inside but it didn't. The room felt moody, dark, and dangerous. The lowered ceilings were painted as black as the nails, eyes, hair, and clothing of most of the patrons.

She had to be in some underground Goth bar. Ignoring the huge, muscled bartender's disapproving stare, she sat on the empty barstool next to the doctor. When she said his name he turned, wide-eyed and looking like he'd just been caught standing over a dead body and holding a smoking gun.

His mouth opened like he was going to speak but only a string of nonsensical gibberish came out. His eyes darted to the bartender and then back to her.

"I'm sorry. I didn't mean to follow you."

"Ch-Ch-Charlotte. What... How..." His throat cleared. "Are you all right?"

"I'm fine. No more fences, I promise." She tried to offer a reassuring smile. Their roles were suddenly reversed and she couldn't imagine why he seemed so nervous. So he liked a little Gothic nightcap. Definitely not something to be ashamed of.

His pleading eyes darted back to the bartender, who nodded and disappeared behind velvet curtains.

"Did you follow me?"

"Sort of. Only inside. I came across this place because..." Now it was her turn to stutter. "I was just outside and saw you walk in. Do you know anything about this house?"

Shaking his head in tiny, jerking movements, he swallowed, and then cleared his throat. "No, but the owner..."

At that, a tall, very scary, very good-looking man approached them. His courteous but reserved smile revealed what looked like vampire teeth. Ones that looked very real and very sharp. "May I help you with something?"

Dr. Anderson immediately rose. "Sorry I can't stay, Charlotte..." He didn't bother to elaborate, quickly ducking out of the bar.

She stared after him. What happened at this place that had him so freaked? Was it a fetish club or something? It didn't matter. She really didn't care.

"You're the owner?" she asked, turning back to the man before her. He was huge, at least six-foot-four—like Xavier, she thought—and she had to crane her neck to look at him. Unlike Xavier, he did not seem eager to entertain her questions.

"Yes. Armand Laroque."

"You've owned the building for a while?"

"It's been in the Laroque family for centuries."

"Oh."

That couldn't be. This was the house, she knew it. Even with the changed décor and layout, she could envision the sitting area where a stage now sat. And the fireplace, now painted black, was exactly where she expected it to be. She could even see Henry standing beside it...

"I just... I've been having these dreams and I thought..." She rubbed her face wearily. "I think I'm going nuts."

She could feel his hazel eyes scrutinizing her. But she wasn't too worried about what a guy with vampire teeth thought of her. "You seem...frazzled. Perhaps we should go back to my office where it's a little quieter. I'd be happy to answer any questions you might have."

"Sure. Why not."

In spite of his menacing look, he didn't make her particularly nervous. A couple of her foster siblings routinely wore "fangs" and they were some of the nicest, coolest people she'd grown up with. A little angsty at times, but so were most foster kids. She certainly wasn't the exception.

It wasn't until the noise of the bar became muted behind thick velvet curtains that she realized if she was here because she truly believed a ghost was haunting her or she was having dreams of a past life, a real life vampire might not be that much of a stretch.

The room they walked through, a room she recognized as the original mudroom, was lined with stacked beer boxes and looked very similar to the backroom of the bar she worked at her freshman year. And the office at the opposite end was just that—a normal, mundane office.

She couldn't imagine a man like him shuffling paper, or answering the phone, or paying invoices...things this desk was obviously designed for. The desk contents might be meticulously stacked and arranged, but they were still normal desk items.

Maybe it was naïve of her to assume his attention to routine office details meant he couldn't possibly be what she thought he was, but she was going to go with it.

The vampire Armand—she snickered a little at that thought—sat behind the desk and invited her to sit opposite in a smooth leather chair. The arrangement was like the office of every psychologist, principle, counselor, or boss she'd ever met.

"Still feel like you're going crazy?"

"More so than ever."

His smile was faint. "What can I do for you Miss...?"

"Boyd. But just call me, Lottie. Um, well..." Now that she was in such a normal environment, away from the Gothic bar patrons, away from the too familiar New Orleans streets, the reason for her coming here seemed too ridiculous to utter.

"You mentioned dreams. Can I assume you're having dreams about my bar?"

"The whole house, really. But I must have been mistaken. The woman I've been dreaming of would have lived here in the early nineteenth century, but you said the house has been in your family for hundreds of years."

"Since shortly after the Battle of New Orleans."

She tried to date the fashion of the people in her dreams. It was very Pride and Prejudice. The timeframe could work out...

"Do you know who owned it before?"

Armand nodded.

"Élise—"

"Cantrelle," he finished for her.

She felt the blood drain from her face and drop into her feet. "Oh my God."

"Not who you were expecting?"

"Exactly who I was expecting." She stared at him with pleading eyes. "I couldn't have known that. I shouldn't have known it."

"The world is rarely what we expect. There are many things beyond...explanation."

With his half-cocked smile she caught a glimpse of his smooth, white fang. His expression was knowing, almost smug.

Oh shit.

She immediately began to back away, keeping her eyes firmly on him. If he moved, even an inch, she was going to bolt. "Thanks for your..." She bumped into the wall and made a quick correction so the open doorway was at her back. "...help. I, um, gotta go."

Leaving her pride and any rational thoughts behind, she turned on her heel and ran, the velvet curtains a brush of heavy silkiness as she shoved through them. Juking around the massive frame of the bartender, she sprinted out the door, down the narrow alleyway and right into Xavier Villere.

She screamed. She couldn't help it. It was like slow-motion movie madness. The noise built in her throat and erupted in all its blood-curdling greatness, in spite of her brain trying to shush it.

"Hey, hey, I got you. Easy." The soft way he

spoke made him sound like he was soothing a spooked horse. And she definitely felt like she could neigh at any minute.

It worked...for the most part. With his strong hands firmly grasping her shoulders and his soothing baritone, she felt her heart slow to a quick jog instead of an all out sprint.

"Are you okay?"

Wasn't that the question of the week.

"Yes. No. God, I don't know. Everything is just so crazy." She tossed a quick, panicked glance over her shoulder. "I gotta get out of here. I don't know if that place is filled with vampires or not but I don't want to find out."

Releasing her from his grasp, Xavier peered over her head. "*La Luxure*? Yeah, it's definitely filled with vamps. They're harmless for the most part."

She missed the feel of his hands on her and was thankful when he took her elbow. "C'mon. I was just about to get a nightcap." He gestured toward the building behind him. "Why don't you join me."

It was her turn to look around him, though his broad shoulders made the task much more difficult. The place he indicated looked like a normal, Irish bar.

She caught his gaze. His deep brown eyes twinkled in the glow from the gas lamps. "Harmless vampires?"

He grinned. "Most of the time."

"Well if they're harmless..."

He started for the bar, gently guiding her. "No worries, they're allergic to Guinness."

"Like garlic?"

"Oh yeah."

They sat at the large wooden bar in the center of the room. Even though the place was busy, the bartender immediately came over to take their order. Beer for Xavier and a vodka/club soda for Lottie. The beer probably would have tasted better but the cocktail was easier to nurse.

It felt good to return to normalcy. The bar, the patrons, the cocktails, Xavier...it all felt natural and Lottie immediately relaxed.

"Better?"

She sighed. "For now."

"It isn't just *La Luxure* that has you so spooked, is it?"

"The vampire bar? No, but going in there certainly didn't help ease my nerves. ."

"It wasn't the tour, was it?" He snorted. "Don't let my brother's blow-hard stories get to you."

"I wish it were that simple." Arms propped onto the bar, she fell into her hands. "I think I'm going crazy. Scratch that. I am going crazy."

He took a long drink of beer. "Aren't we all."

"Not like this. This is certifiable."

She peered at him from the corners of her eyes. God, he was gorgeous, a mixture of several ethnicities that blended into exotic perfection. His nose and jaw chiseled and strong, his lips full and very soft looking, his black eyes framed by even thicker, black lashes, his skin...like coffee and cream. Beautiful.

She swallowed. "Like, lock-me-up-certifiable," she went on, unsure why she was even telling him that detail.

Her statement didn't faze him. In fact, it seemed to capture his interest. Twisting in his seat to look squarely at her, he perched on an elbow and leaned against the bar. "How so?"

"I don't know that I even want to say it out loud. It's just... It's just nuts."

"You met Julien. He's completely normal compared to the rest of my family." Xavier laughed. "You don't have to tell me if you don't want to…"

She could tell by his tone he definitely wanted her to. Should she…?

"I'm having these dreams," she blurted. She wasn't sure why, but something about the way he looked at her, like he wanted to peel back all her layers and dive into her core. It wasn't something she wanted to deny. "Vivid dreams set in New Orleans with historic details I couldn't possibly know."

Unfortunately, that made him frown. He took a drink. "What kind of details?"

"Well, like doctors used to prescribe calomel to sick patients. It's basically mercury and makes you puke. I'd never heard of it before I dreamt about it. I had to look it up."

"Maybe you just don't remember learning about it."

"It's more than that. The clothes, the buildings, the customs, the bloodletting… I saw the tool used to puncture the vein perfectly in my mind. Again, I had to look it up, but it was exactly as I'd seen it."

He took another drink, his frown deepening. "Those are all details you could have learned in elementary school. You could have forgotten and then our historic NOLA streets just gave fuel for your imagination to run."

For someone so interested in her secret minutes earlier, he sure seemed quick to deny it. "I saw Sanite Villere in my dreams. Long before I'd ever seen her portrait in your shop."

"Well, that—"

"Lottie! Oh my God!" Amanda's shrill voice shattered Xavier's sentence.

Amanda, Sam, and much to Lottie's surprise, Julien, stood in the doorway. Amanda hustled over and threw her arms around her neck. "You got my text! I'm so glad you made it!" When drunk, Amanda had a tendency to get really affectionate.

Lottie had no idea if she'd gotten a text or not but she nodded anyway. "Of course," she said, trying not to swallow a lock of Amanda's hair. She glanced over at Xavier, but he was focused on his brother.

Julien had his arm around Sam and they were stumbling toward the bar. Judging from the glazed look in Sam's eyes and the way her eyelids hung heavily over them, she was wasted.

"Hey, look who it is!" Julien exclaimed, his voice just a little slurred. "My little cutter! You put on quite a show tonight. People loved it. They couldn't stop talking about you. Added a little extra to my tips, too." He winked. "I'll buy you a drink."

"Yeah, shouldn't...shouldn't you be in the psych ward or something?" Sam swayed as she asked the question. Her words weren't just a little slurred either. *Something* came out as *thomthing*.

Amanda finally released her. "Sam..." she said tensely.

Xavier glanced briefly at Lottie before asking his brother, "What are you talking about?"

Lottie was pretty sure she'd like to disappear. She might have been willing to tell him what happened in the cemetery but not here, not like this. Not with *this* audience.

Besides, Sam had that hateful look in her eyes she sometimes got when she drank. The prospect for a quiet rest of the night wasn't looking good.

"Didn't she tell you?" Julien laughed, shaking Sam from his side. She stumbled without the support.

Clasping Xavier on the shoulder, he jabbed his thumb at Lottie. "We're in the cemetery, everything's cool, and I look over and crazy here has sliced the shit out of her hand with a nail file and is walking all zombie-like toward some grave. Amanda had to restrain her."

Xavier turned to her, his expression a mixture of concern and apprehension. Lottie was immediately reminded of the man Élise ran into on the street, the one who warned her about the calomel.

With a sigh she held up her bandaged hand. "Told you I was losing my mind."

Julien just laughed. Expression hard, Xavier looked like he was ramping up to retort when Sam crashed between them, nearly knocking over his beer. He snatched it up just in time.

"Hey, let's do a shot," she slurred. "Not Lottie, cause she's a fucking fun-sponge, but I know you're fun." She said to Julien. "I'm not sure 'bout you," she said, turning to Xavier. "But you're hot so I'm sure you're fun."

And cue the train-wreck...

Lottie rose. "You know, I think I'll go." She wasn't sure where since she wasn't going back to their hotel room alone, but she had to be somewhere else. "Thanks for the drink and the company," she said quietly to Xavier. Raising her voice, she added in the gentlest voice possible, "Hey Sam, you wanna head back with me?"

Sam's face contorted into an ugly mess that defied her normally gorgeous face. "Fuck no!" She turned to Julien. "See, told you. Fucking fun-sponge."

Lottie felt her jaw tighten and her fists clench into balls. She closed her eyes. She shouldn't let Sam get to her. She was just drunk. Normally she wasn't such a bitch.

But she was a bitch a lot.

"You aren't going to go all nutzoid again are you? Hide your nail files everyone!" Sam's shrill laughter was even louder than her voice—a drunken four decibels too high.

Amanda linked her elbow around Lottie's and began to lead her away. "C'mon. Let's go to the bathroom."

She didn't resist, especially when she caught sight of Xavier's expression. He was looking at her like she might burst into flames at any moment. She was happy to get the hell out of there, even if it was only to escape into a dirty bathroom.

"Ignore Sam," Amanda said when the door closed behind them. "She's being a total asshat."

"I know. I just gotta get out of here. I can't take it. Not tonight." Lottie's gaze drifted toward the sink. Remembering the creepiness from the hotel room and the reason she was out and about at three-thirty a.m., she shuddered.

Amanda stroked her arm. "You okay?"

She turned away from the faucet. "No," she admitted. She definitely was not okay. "I'm scared to go back. I can't be in that hotel room alone."

"I'll go with you. I've been the third wheel ever since Julien hooked up with Sam after the tour. I'm effin' beat anyway."

When she nodded her head felt so heavy she was surprised her neck didn't snap under the strain. God, she was exhausted. Mentally, physically, emotionally...just exhausted. Every muscle in her body felt weak, ruined, and in desperate need of a nice warm bubble bath. Not that she wanted to go anywhere near the hotel bathroom...

"Do you think we can sneak out without being

seen?" She didn't want to face Sam again, or Julien, or Xavier. Especially not Xavier. Maybe she shouldn't care if he looked at her like her head was going to do a three-sixty, or she was going to start levitating, but she did.

"I'm sure we can. Lemme just pee real fast and we'll bail..."

They didn't exactly escape without being seen, but Amanda simply kept moving when Sam hollered at them. She tossed Sam a quick wave and then practically shoved Lottie out the door and down the sidewalk toward their hotel.

"She's going to be so pissed at you," Lottie said.

Amanda shrugged. "I doubt she'll remember. But if she does I'll just tell her I was going to hurl if we didn't go."

The walk back was uneventful. Amanda rattled on about her evening and Lottie was happy for the distraction of her bar-tales. In some ways, she wished she had it in her to let loose and dance on the stripper pole like Amanda, or even hook up with guys as easily as Sam. Just be a normal college student on spring break.

But she wasn't. And probably never would be again. She hadn't been normal since her parents died. She never let loose anymore, couldn't let loose. Forever guarded, the walls she put up wouldn't let her. She certainly couldn't have normal relationships— with friends or with men.

The suite was quiet and empty, just as she had left it. Amanda headed straight for the back bedroom, flopping on the bed and tossing her purse on the nightstand. "Hey, you care if I crash in here with you."

Actually, she preferred it. Sleeping alone was low on her list of desires.

"Not at all."

"Good. I get the feeling Julien and Sam are going to come back here and I'd rather not have to listen to them doing the nasty..."

Lottie climbed onto the bed on the opposite side of Amanda, who was kicking off her shoes. "Two guys in one day. That can't be safe."

Amanda shrugged. "Well, at least there was a few hours and a shower between them. 'Sides, she always uses protection."

"Still..." Lottie mentally took back her passing desire to be able to hook up with men as easily as Sam.

Amanda's phone buzzed. She fished it out of her purse, read something on the screen, chuckled, and then typed a quick reply before dropping the phone onto the nightstand.

"What's so funny?"

Without undressing or changing, Amanda slid under the covers. "Sam's actually concerned we got home safely. Weird. Well, g'night Lotts."

"Goodnight."

Like a switch had been flipped, within minutes Amanda was lightly snoring.

The sound was soothing. After locking the bedroom door (last thing she wanted was for Sam and Julien to stumble into their bedroom) and changing back into her Pajamas, she took one final look around the empty room and then clicked off the lamp.

Happy to have Amanda's warm body beside her, she quickly fell asleep.

CHAPTER SEVEN

Sam's drunken slur grated heavily on Xavier's nerves, making him cringe with every high-pitched squeal. She was blathering on about something barely coherent, but the last thing he cared to do was pay attention long enough to figure out what she was saying. God help Julien if he decided to bring that plastic bimbo to their family home. At least the Guest House was vacant—in the middle of a renovation not scheduled to be completed until shortly before Jazz Fest.

His gaze was fixated on the closed door to the women's restroom where Amanda had scurried off with Lottie. He didn't know what to think of the situation. Even for all her admissions of lunacy, he didn't peg her for a cutter, or an attention seeker. Whatever was going on with her, she seemed genuinely confused by it. And she definitely believed it.

He hated dwelling on anything remotely paranormal. From Grandmere's potions and Voodoo rituals, to his mother's fortune telling and spirit channeling, to his family legacy, to the contents of his store, he was constantly around the idea of the supernatural. And he didn't believe any of it.

But he too had dreams. Well, really just one. The same one. Over and over.

The door to the women's restroom opened and Amanda, then Lottie, still looking shell-shocked, emerged. Her beautiful face was lined with worry, her blue eyes haunted. He wished he'd had more time with her before the hurricane that now surrounded him crashed through the door.

As much as he hated the occult, he wanted to know what she'd seen, what she'd experienced, why her delicate brows pushed so fiercely together, why she chewed nervously on her bottom lip as the pair skirted the edge of the bar. It was pretty obvious they were trying to escape without being seen.

The plastic-haired drunk hanging from his brother's arm was part of the problem, he knew that, but she was only a small part. Lottie's demons went much deeper.

He rose, ready to meet them at the door. He might not know for sure how he felt about her claims or how to react to them, but he knew how he felt about her. Whether it was pure surface attraction or just fascination, she called to him and he needed to know more. Besides, he wasn't going to let two women traipse around the Quarter unaccompanied at this late hour. The vampires at *Luxure* might be mostly harmless, but they weren't completely harmless. And they weren't the only dangers in this town.

Sam screeched at them and he cringed. Amanda waved and then they disappeared from the bar.

Time to go.

He started forward but was stopped by Julien's hand around his arm. He stared at the hand and then at his brother. "What are you doing?"

"I should ask you the same thing." There was something off about his voice.

Xavier tried to pull his arm away but Julien held fast.

"You seriously aren't going after that crazy broad," he said. Once again, his voice sounded...wrong somehow, but Xavier couldn't pinpoint why.

"I'm just walking them back to their hotel. Why the fuck do you care?"

"You can't be with her."

"Who says I'm trying to *be* with anyone." He attempted to pull his arm away again, with a little more force this time, but still failed. "Jesus, would you let go already."

Julien stepped forward until his face was inches from Xavier's. Fuck, his eyes...they glistened with pure hate.

"She's crazy. She's cursed. She'll bring you nothing but misery and pain."

Speaking of crazy...

Or just fucking wasted.

Without restraint this time, Xavier shoved his brother back and jerked his arm away. Julien fell into the bar, knocking over a beer in the process. He blinked a couple times.

"What the hell...?"

Xavier didn't wait around. Pushing through the crowded bar and onto the sidewalk, he quickly swept the street in each direction for Amanda and Lottie. They were gone. Of course. Dumbass Julien pretty much guaranteed that.

Assuming their hotel was one of the many in the

heart of the Quarter, he jogged down St. Philip, scanning Royal as he passed, hoping to spot Lottie's mane of blond curls in the darkness. Nothing. The street was virtually vacant.

He turned onto Bourbon and continued as far as Orleans where the crowd on the street made it pointless to continue. He had no idea if he was headed the right direction anyway. They could be staying on Frenchman for all he knew.

Chasing after them might be futile, but he'd kick his own ass from here to Sunday if something happened to them. Right after he kicked Julien's ass. He needed to know they at least made it back safely. He'd figure out what he needed to know about Lottie later.

With a grimace, he headed back to the Irish bar. Luckily the plastic bimbo was still glued to his brother's arm. Somehow, she was not only still standing, but even drunker than before.

"Call your friends," he said.

Her head swayed unsteadily from side to side as she turned to him, not a single drop of recognition in her unfocused eyes.

"What are you doing back here?" Julien asked.

"I wasn't talking to you," he replied without taking his eyes off Sam. "Call your friends."

"Huh?"

"Call. Your. Friends. Amanda...Lottie."

"Why?"

"Just do it."

She fumbled through her purse, pulling out various items and setting them on the bar—lipstick, a compact, her wallet, some tissues—until she finally found her phone. With a smile that suggested she'd found gold instead of a phone, she held it up.

He waited...impatiently, and she just looked at him. After a few agonizing seconds, he took the phone from her. It was possible he actually yanked it from her, but he liked to think he gently removed it from her hands.

It wouldn't be the first time he'd lied to himself.

"Hey!"

He ignored her.

There was an unread text message from Amanda. Good enough. Hitting reply, he wrote, *You make it home okay?*

While waiting for the response, he sifted through her contacts, finding Lottie's number and committing it to memory.

The phone chirped and he shifted back to text messages. It was Amanda...thank God.

Ha! You are fucking drunk! Yes, we're here. Try not to lose your keycard.

He passed the phone to Sam. She snatched it back.

Without a parting word, he turned and left. He'd gotten what he needed. Lottie—-and Amanda—were safely back at their hotel.

The moment he walked through the door to his house, Xavier knew something wasn't right. The door to the ritual room was closed and he could clearly hear voices coming form the other side. He didn't normally pay much attention to the séances, cleansing rituals, or whatever other mumbo jumbo his female relatives were engaged in. But it was four a.m. Why on earth would his mother or Grandmere have clients at this hour?

Listening carefully, he realized it was only Grandmere. He decided to ignore it, as he normally did. She had more than earned the right to have her own personal ritual any time she desired. Even at four a.m.

That and he was dog tired and ready to put the night behind him. He still regretted allowing Lottie to escape without his escort. Thankfully her dumbass friend had been able to text him or he would have had to check every room in their hotel to make sure she was safe. Or comb the streets until he found them. Or sleep in the hotel foyer like some crazed stalker until they arrived.

Now, sleep was all he could think about.

Grandmere's chanting became louder, interrupting his thoughts. Ears pricked, he crept toward the door. He'd been wrong. It wasn't just her.

What the hell was she thinking? Having late night clients was not only crazy, but could be dangerous. At least during normal hours, someone was usually around in case things went badly. But now? She was completely vulnerable.

Rattled but not so unsettled to interrupt, he pressed his ear to the door. At first, only her familiar chant greeted him, but then another voice replaced it. Deeper, gravelly, male.

He cracked the door. Cloudy eyes stared straight at him. Sweat covered her body, soaking her clothes. Tendrils of gray dreadlocks clung to her saturated skin. Though she stood perfectly still, he could see the rise and fall of her chest, like she'd recently been engaged in some very vigorous dancing.

"Come in child," the unfamiliar male voice slid from her familiar mouth.

He pushed the door open wider, keeping his feet firmly in the other room, and scanned the room. Besides an intricate symbol drawn with sand on the floor, nothing in the room was out of place and she was alone.

"Are you all right?"

"She is lost," the male voice replied. "She needs your help. You must trust her. Only she holds the key."

Okay, he had to be mistaken. That voice couldn't come from the old woman before him. But there wasn't anyone else, at least not anyone visible.

"She is trapped. You must trust her. You must help her."

"Grandmere…?"

She continued to stare at him with her unseeing eyes. There was something foreign about them. In fact, her entire expression was foreign, like it belonged to another face.

"Grandmere," he said more firmly.

Silence. Had she even heard his words? There was nothing in her reaction to indicate she had. A pit formed in his stomach and he suddenly feared for her mental safety. Maybe all the years of believing this crap had finally gotten to her.

Pushing to door wide he strode toward her and gently took her shoulders. "Grandmere," he repeated in an even firmer voice, his face directly in front of hers. "It's me, Xavier. Talk to me. Are you okay?"

She blinked a few time times and then took a deep breath, her expression returning to normal. The knot in his stomach relaxed. Releasing his grip on her, he retrieved a glass from the buffet, filled it with water from the neighboring pitcher, and placed it into her hands. Her gnarled and knotted fingers wrapped around it and she took a drink.

"Thank you." Her voice wavered.

"Everything okay? You had me scared there for a

moment."

"Why, what happened?" Her trembling hand set the glass back on the buffet.

"You were talking. Don't you remember?"

"Of course not. No one ever remembers when they're possessed by Loa."

Resisting the urge to roll his eyes, he set his jaw. "Grandmere, please be serious."

"I am serious. You are the one in denial," she chided. "It isn't my fault you can't see your nose in front of your face."

The eye rolling was even harder to resist.

"What did I say?"

"Just gibberish."

"Just because you think it's gibberish, don't mean I will. What did I say, boy?" Her eyes, even though they were so clouded they were a mass of white, focused intently on him, letting him know she meant business.

"Something about being trapped, and trusting her, and helping her, and freeing her." She hadn't said the last part so he wasn't sure why he added it.

"Oh." She seemed disappointed. "Why would he say that?" she added in a quiet voice obviously meant for her ears only.

The mention of a man piqued his interest. "He? Who is he?"

"Go to bed, Xavier. It ain't important."

Five minutes ago he would have taken her advice, went to bed and forgotten it. Now, he had to know. "It is important. You were speaking in a man's voice. Who were you trying to channel?"

"Papa Legba."

He had to strain his brain to remember who Papa Legba was besides a Talking Heads song. Oh, right, the gatekeeper to the spirit world, Legba was the Loa one must contact before they can access the dead.

"Who were you trying to contact?"

"It don't matter. Go to bed." As sharp as her tone was, there was also an undeniable sadness to her words.

"Of course it matters," he said softly. "It always matters."

"Your stupid grandfather. Why he had to up and have a heart attack after I begged him over and over to quit the drink and the smokes and the bacon. Stubborn. Just like you. Now go to bed before I have to drag you there myself."

Well, at least she was back to normal. And obviously wanted to be alone. A request he intended to honor.

"If you insist." He kissed her cheek and she swatted at him like he was an annoying gnat. "Goodnight."

As he climbed the stairs to his room, he heard her muttering to herself. Thankfully, in her own voice.

CHAPTER EIGHT

It was an agonizing hour before Rosette returned, during which Élise worked nonstop to cool Amélie's fever. By the time she heard the front door open, Amélie's sheets were drenched and Élise wasn't sure if it was from sweat or from the water she continuously dripped onto her skin.

She wasn't sure what to expect and her heart leapt into a frenzy of anticipation. Especially as she heard two sets of footsteps on the curving staircase. The creak of wood on the third stair from the top made her jump out of her chair.

A stranger was in her house, not just a stranger to her home but a witch doctor—a man who routinely practiced the dark arts.

She crossed herself just before they stepped through the door.

"Oh!" she gasped when she saw the tall, broad-shouldered, handsome man with caramel colored skin standing beside Rosette. It was the man she'd run into the previous day, the man who had helped her retrieve her fallen items, the man whose grip was both powerful and gentle.

A man who wore a smile that was both reassuring and warm.

He bowed his head. "It's a pleasure to meet you formally, Madame Cantrelle. It is unfortunate that it must be under these circumstances. I am Laurent Villere."

"Oh my God." Lottie sat up with a jerk, the mattress creaking and groaning with the sudden movement.

The witch doctor was a Villere. The man on the street—the one who had helped Élise, who was, hopefully, going to help Amélie—was a Villere. They were connected, Laurent and Xavier.

She tossed the covers aside. She had to go to the store. She had to see Xavier. Now.

But it was still dark, really dark. Not trusting it wasn't noon and the hotel blinds were tricking her, she rose and lifted the brocade drapes. Nope, still dark. There was a glimmer of sunlight cresting in the distance but it wasn't enough to dictate she rush down to a store that wouldn't be open for hours.

She wished she had Xavier's number. But even if she did she couldn't call him. It'd make her seem even crazier. The first opportunity though, she was going down there. Until then…?

What should she do? Surely Élise Cantrelle wasn't her enemy. Was Laurent Villere? What about Sanite, Xavier, Julien...?

If she wanted the answers, she knew she needed to go back to sleep. That was easier said than done. There was no way she'd be able to fall asleep now. Her nerves were a firestorm of activity, her muscles twitched, and her heart pounded at the excitement of the discovery.

She stared into the courtyard. The pool was a sheet of smooth blue glass. Beyond that a lion spewed a waterfall into the fountain.

Where had Xavier gone after the encounter at the Irish bar? Had he stayed, had a few shots with Sam and Julien? Joked about what a nut she was?

She could envision the scene with perfect clarity. Glasses clinking with broad smiles, they laughed about her meekness, her social awkwardness, her sudden cutter tendencies. Ghosts? Lottie sees ghosts? Yeah, and probably her dead parents too.

She sighed. Her own ridiculous insecurities were clouding the real issue. In spite of what her apprehensive brain might think, she was being haunted. She was certain of it. And yet, she was fixated on what Xavier Villere may or may not have done.

Although obviously the two obsessions were somehow related. Maybe that's why she was so drawn to him. Maybe that's why she kept thinking about him.

Releasing the curtain, she turned back to the room. Amanda slept soundly, her even breathing and soft snoring like a metronome.

Lottie sighed, suddenly jealous of Amanda's unconscious state. She needed to be asleep too. It was the only way to fill in the missing pieces. But how…?

Her eyes finally adjusted to the darkness, she caught sight of Amanda's purse on the nightstand. Of course. Amanda was a bit of a pill popper and had quite the pharmacy in her purse. A pharmacy that included sleeping pills—heavy duty ones at that. The type that could only be prescribed, were highly addictive, and had weird side effects like sleep walking, or sometimes in Amanda's case, sleep sexing.

No matter, it was exactly what Lottie needed. Creeping to the nightstand, she carefully peeled open the purse and began fishing bottles out one by one, using the light from the alarm clock to read the names until she finally found the right one.

Opening the bottle sounded like gears grinding through metal and pouring the pills into her hand like boulders crashing down a mountainside, but Amanda didn't stir. Lottie really only needed one pill, but grabbed a few extra, just in case. Ignoring the pangs of guilt she felt for stealing, she gulped down a pill with a swig from the open bottle of water next to the clock. After zipping the remaining pills into the coin pocket of her purse, she carefully climbed back into bed, like a husband trying not to wake his wife after returning from a night at the strip club.

Pulling the covers up to her chin, she closed her eyes and waited for the pill to do its magic. She didn't have to wait long.

"Thank you so much for coming, Monsieur Villere. I just don't know what else to do."

"May I see the child?"

"Of course." Élise stepped aside and he wasted no time moving to Amélie's side. Kneeling by her bed, he placed a hand gently on her face. His skin, while no darker than a fisherman's or farmer's at the end of summer, contrasted sharply against her ivory complexion—made even paler by the burning fever.

He lifted his gaze to hers. His rich, brown eyes sparkled in the flickering light from the oil lamp. She was shocked by how beautiful she found him. His thick black hair topped his strong face in silky looking waves longing to be touched.

"I'd like to start with a healing tonic. It should help bring her fever down." His eyes flicked past Élise. "Rosette, please bring me the red bottle."

Holding a sealed, ceramic, long-necked bottle, the servant scampered past her and handed it to Laurent. Gently and oh so slowly, he lifted Amélie up. She was like a rag-doll in his arms and Élise felt her heart tighten until she was sure it stopped beating. It was only when Amélie groaned a little, twisting in Laurent's strong arms that she felt it renew its rhythmic dance.

"Shhh," he soothed, stroking her sweat-soaked hair. "Cheri," he whispered. "You will be well." He held the bottle up and Rosette removed the cork. "Drink this," he said, coaxing the bottle mouth between Amélie's tiny, perfect lips. "It is sweet, like candy."

He tipped the bottle back and when the liquid first dribbled down Amélie's chin, Élise wondered if her little girl would be strong enough to even swallow. But Laurent pulled the bottle back, allowing a small drop to land on her tongue. It took a few moments but soon, Amélie languidly licked the elixir from her lips.

"That's good." Her voice was like the weak mewl of a newborn kitten.

Laurent's smile lit up the room. "It is. Have some more." More liquid dripped from the bottle and once again Amélie lapped at it. The process continued for some time. With the utmost care, he offered the tonic and waited for her to consume it until the bottle was empty.

Élise was amazed how patient, how gentle he

was. Not once did his deep voice rise in volume and he handled her daughter with such care...it made her heart happy and sad at the same time.

When the tonic was gone, he eased Amélie back onto the bed and turned to Élise waiting expectantly. "What now?" she asked.

That smile again, oh that smile.

"The tonic alone should help, but if you like..." He paused. "Only if you are comfortable..."

She knew what he was inferring. "Anything," she said.

Perhaps she should worry for the sake of her soul by agreeing to partake in his magic, but she would gladly face hell if it meant Amélie would rise from that bed.

"In Voodoo," Laurent began, "it is believed the spirits of our loved ones watch over us and help keep us safe. Is there a spirit we could appease to help protect and heal her?"

"Her father."

He nodded, his dark eyes a mirror of understanding. "Do you have a portrait of him?"

"I do."

"Can you please bring it to me?"

"I'll get it, Madame," Rosette said.

"No, Rosette. I need you to help prepare the altar."

"I'll go," Élise said quickly. "It's no trouble."

She scurried down the hall and into the sitting room. Hanging over the mantle was Nathanael's portrait, painted right before their wedding, still watching over his family like the strong patriarch he'd been. He was such a handsome man, usually kind, not much of a temper...

They'd been happy. Certainly with their share of

problems, but happy nonetheless.

Gripping the bottom edge of the frame, she carefully lifted the portrait from its mount and carried it back up the stairs.

"I'm afraid this is the smallest I have," she said as she entered the room.

Laurent was placing two white candles on top of the chest now covered with a rich velvet cloth. He turned at the sound of her voice and immediately relieved her of the burden of carrying the large painting.

"It will do just fine," he said, setting the frame on the chest and leaning it against the wall so that Nathanael looked over the daughter he'd never met.

A shrine. Laurent had built a shrine.

He placed a small wicker basket directly in front of the painting and then lit the candles and a small bundle of sage. Smoke smoldering from the herb, he paced the room, waving it back and forth while he chanted. She didn't recognize the words, but she did recognize the dialect. It was the language newly arrived slaves often uttered when they first stepped off the boats.

Chanting the entire time, he diligently covering every inch of the room until the fragrant smoke hung in all corners. His deep voice was soothing, calming.

Leaning against the doorjamb and resting her head on the wood, she closed her eyes to enjoy its cadence. It was the first time she'd felt at peace in a long time. The smell of the sage, the sound of his rich voice, the presence of the very man...she felt relaxed, even with the chaos of Amélie's sickness.

The chanting stopped. When she opened her eyes, he was placing the extinguished sage into the basket and then added a few coins. "Do you have anything to offer the spirit?" he asked, turning to her.

Feeling shameful for reveling in the pleasure of his voice, she pushed stiffly off the jamb. "Um..." What could she offer? "Oh!" With quick fingers, she removed her earrings and placed them into the basket. "Will these do?" she wondered, twisting to look up at him.

His body was closer than she'd realized. Close enough she could practically feel the heat radiating from his strong body. Close enough she could smell the lovely fragrance of his cologne. Close enough she could fully appreciate his broad male chest, the strength in his hands, the way his eyes smoldered when he looked at her.

She would have backed away but she was trapped between the chest and the wall, trapped between the heat of his body and the heat of his gaze.

"They are perfect," he said quietly. "Spirits like gifts, offerings. It makes them strong. I have asked him to watch over your daughter, to protect her from the illness that ravages her. Hopefully he listens."

She could only nod, the inside of her bottom lip pinched tightly between her teeth.

"One more thing." He retrieved an item from the basket Rosette had carried up the stairs and hung it on the headboard above Amélie's pale head.

"A chicken's foot?"

He smiled. "A talisman of protection."

"Oh..."

He approached her again but kept a respectable distance this time. She found she preferred the former.

"I'm afraid there isn't much else for me to do," he said.

"I cannot thank you enough for coming, Monsieur Villere."

"It was my pleasure."

"I can pay you. Just let me get my purse." She turned to leave but his voice stopped her.

"That won't be necessary."

She felt her brows push together. *"But I must pay you for your services."*

"I could never accept payment while the patient is still an invalid."

Her brows did not relax. *"Perhaps..."*

He held a broad, dark hand out. *"I insist."*

"When she is fully recovered then?" At that thought, Élise felt her brow relax. In fact, she felt a tiny pull at the corners of her lips.

His smile wasn't quite so small. *"Very well, you may call on me when she has recovered."*

"Accepted." She offered her hand in handshake. With a grin, he accepted, and she did her best to seal their bargain like a man.

Even after the handshake was sufficient, she found her hand lingered in his. She meant to draw it back immediately, as was proper, but the sensation of his flesh against her own felt too good, too perfect to pull away.

Nor did he attempt to withdraw. His grip on her hand did loosen, but only so his fingers could slide free until her hand was cupped in his.

She didn't know what to do. She didn't want to move, or break the contact, but she couldn't stand there and stare at him.

His thumb brushed the top of her hand in a caress so gentle, yet so mesmerizing, she wanted to close her eyes and just disappear into it.

The thought alone should make her pull away. She didn't.

"Shall I escort Monsieur—Oh!"

Immediately releasing each other's hand, they both turned, startled, toward the door. Rosette stood in the opening, a tiny grin on her full lips.

Straightening, she cleared her throat. "I'll go..."

"No," Élise interjected. "That won't be necessary. Yes, you may escort Monsieur Villere out."

"Are you certain?"

Élise gave her a warning look and though she tried to be subtle, she knew she probably failed miserably. Laurent was enough of a gentleman he did not mention it when she turned back to him, and his neutral expression told her he was even more of a gentleman.

"Again, thank you so much for the house-call, Monsieur Villere. Please accept my sincerest appreciation."

"It was my honor," he said with a bow. He turned to Rosette. "I am ready to take my leave."

"If you will follow me, sir." The words were proper, but her expression was anything but.

Élise's hard stare followed her until she disappeared from view.

Once they were gone, every ounce of tension held in her body abruptly fled. Her knees sank and she braced against the armoire.

The energy buzzing through her body...she hadn't reacted that way to the touch of a man in ages. Or perhaps never. She had loved Nathanael deeply, but their affair was not a passionate one.

Shaking it off, she went to the bed and knelt over Amélie. This was hardly the time to be entertaining such thoughts about a man she barely knew. Even one as kind, handsome, and gentle as Laurent Villere.

Tentatively, she placed a hand on her daughter's forehead. She felt...cooler. Her skin still warm but no longer scalding. Was it possible? Had her fever broken?

"Oh Madame, I am so sorry I interrupted."

Élise straightened stiffly and turned. "You interrupted nothing."

Rosette gave her a coy glance.

"You forget yourself," Élise said sternly. But she couldn't keep up the act and broke into a smile. "Amélie's fever may have broken!"

Rosette joined her at the bed. After testing the child's temperature, she concurred.

"I don't want to be so presumptuous to get ahead of myself, but I pray, I hope..." Élise cleared her throat and took the servant's hands. Looking the woman straight in the eyes she added, "Thank you for fetching Monsieur Villere. I think he may be just what we needed."

Rosette's coy smile returned. "I don't doubt that for one second."

CHAPTER NINE

There was no denying the daylight when Lottie woke up later that morning. The darkest light canceling drapes couldn't hide the bright rays of sunlight streaming into the room.

Her head felt heavy and ached dully, like someone had squeezed Play-Doh into her ears while she slept and was now pounding it with a rubber mallet.

Those were some drugs Amanda kept in her arsenal. She was pretty sure they could knock out a horse. She made a mental note to take half a pill next time. If there needed to be a next time.

With jelly arms, she pushed herself into an upright position and tried to focus on something other than the slush between her ears. Amanda wasn't in the room, she could start with that. Of course, that didn't mean much. It could be nine a.m. or it could be two p.m. or noon the following day and she'd just slept really long and Amanda had hooked up with someone.

Flopping onto her elbow, she squinted to get a good look at the alarm clock. It read One-fifteen. It wasn't the worst scenario. So she'd slept—like a corpse—through the morning. At least Villere House would be open and hopefully Xavier would be there. With everything she'd learned during the hours spent unconscious, she needed to get to him more than ever.

She now knew for sure that neither Élise nor Laurent were her enemies. She still didn't know what the ghost wanted or needed from her, but she sure as hell knew where to start looking.

Shoving the comforter aside, she staggered out of bed and to the bathroom, quickly splashing cold water on her face and brushing her teeth, still wary of letting the water run too long. Removing the funk from her mouth and shocking her skin with frigid liquid eased her pill-induced fog a little. The rest of the urgency to get to Villere House as soon as possible came from somewhere deep in her gut. The answers she sought would be found there, she was sure of it.

Why she was so driven to find those answers...well, that wasn't a question she could answer. They were leaving tomorrow and she was pretty sure the weird dreams she'd been having would stay behind in New Orleans. In fact, in twenty-four hours she'd be well on her way back to Kirksville. She could leave all of this weirdness behind her.

The thought made her physically sick.

And filled her with an even stronger need to get to Villere House. Now.

With a new sense of urgency and a slightly clearer head, she threw on clean undies, a fresh tank, and a pair of shorts that were just a hair too short. Flip-flops rounded out her outfit. Grabbing her small, over the shoulder purse, she shoved through the door, crossing the courtyard before the door had a chance to close.

Even though she couldn't begin to describe where

the Voodoo shop was, she didn't have to pull up the map once. Without thinking, without hesitation, she marched straight there and into the store.

Sitting on a tall stool behind the counter and ringing up a customer, Xavier stood up the moment he saw her.

"I have to talk to you."

"Sure." Without taking his eyes off her, he ripped the receipt from the credit card machine and handed it and a pen to the waiting woman.

It seemed to take her an eon to sign the receipt and hand it back to him.

"Thanks for coming in." His eyes flicked briefly to the woman to pass over her purchase before returning his gaze to Lottie.

She should have felt nervous under his stare but she only felt impatient. Ready for this woman to leave so she could have his undivided attention.

He followed the woman as she left the store, locking the door behind her. "What's going on?" he asked as he turned.

Okay, now she felt nervous. She may have wanted his full attention but now that there was no chance of an interruption, no chance of a distraction, her heart fluttered erratically.

"Laurent Villere," she blurted.

His brow furrowed. "My great…grandfather. What about him?"

"Remember I told you I was having weird dreams, dreams about people and things I shouldn't know about?"

"Yeah."

"Well I dreamed about Laurent."

"You've been in the store. You went on a Voodoo tour..."

"And he was never mentioned! I only know the name because in my dreams he was called on to heal Amélie." He raised an eyebrow. "Élise Cantrelle's sick daughter." The eyebrow went higher.

The desire to tell him everything suddenly became more urgent, the desire to have him understand sheer desperation. Before she'd thought she was crazy and didn't care if he shared that sentiment. Now though, she knew she wasn't crazy. She was haunted.

She didn't dare look at him as it gushed from her like a waterfall. Everything. From Élise being spooked by Sanite Villere and running into Laurent on the street, to the long night of relentless vomiting poor Amélie endured as a result of the calomel, to the horrible doctor and the bloodletting, to Laurent coming and hopefully saving the day. She even told him about hearing her name called while showering, and seeing Élise on the sidewalk, following her to the cemetery and almost being killed, to cutting herself at the grave. When she finished, out of breath and feeling like she'd been fleeing a pack of wolves, she was finally able to look at him.

His expression looked purposefully neutral, like he was trying desperately to keep the judgment from his face.

She felt strangely defeated. "You don't believe me, do you?"

"I don't know."

"I'm not making it up."

"I didn't think you were. I just don't know that it's what you think it is."

"What else could it be?"

He shook his head, perplexed.

"I can describe him. Laurent. Even if I were

95

imagining the rest, I know his face. He's tall, like you. Same dark eyes. Skin's a little darker. A more Native American nose, strong jaw, fuller lips. His hair is black, wavy, styled kind-of Romanesque." She saw the recognition flash in his eyes. "How would I know these things? It's not like he's in the history books, or there's a portrait of him hanging around."

He pursed his lips.

"There is a portrait! So you know I've described him perfectly!"

"Yes, but..."

"But what?" She needed him to believe her. As much as she needed to breathe, she needed him on her side. "Okay what about Élise Cantrelle? How would I know her? How would I know the vampire bar used to be her home? How would I know what she looked like? Blond, with curly hair, kind-of like mine—"

Oh God, why hadn't she thought of it before? Could that be why Élise was haunting her?

She stared at Xavier. "Do you think we're related? Élise and I?"

"Possible. Don't you know?"

"I have no idea. I don't know anything about my family." It was a fact she was painfully aware of, but saying it aloud made her sad.

"Isn't there someone you can ask?"

She shook her head. "My parents both died when I was fifteen. And they were both only children, like me. My grandparents have all been dead for years. And as far as the State could figure out, there's no one else." She shook her head again.

"I'm sorry."

"It is what it is."

"Well, that sounds like a place to start then. Tulane has an extensive library. Even though I graduated last year, my student I.D. should still work. And if it doesn't, I have a friend who works there. We should be able to find out if you're related to Élise Cantrelle."

"You want to help me?"

"Of course."

"But if you don't believe me, why would you help me?"

"Because this is obviously important to you, and I can tell it's upsetting. Anything I can do to help you find the answers you're looking for, I'll do."

"Okay, let's start at the beginning. Élise..."

"Cantrelle," she finished. "She would have lived at the vampire bar. On St. Philip." Because there might be another vampire bar...

"Year?"

"Early 19th century. The clothing is very Pride and Prejudice."

He smiled. "Okay, let me see if there's a Jane Austen setting..."

"Oh, they'd just built the Presbyterian church on St. Charles."

"Well, that'd be—oh, here she is."

"Really?" Lottie leaned over his shoulder to peer at the computer screen, bracing her hand on his solid, rather well defined, trapezius muscle. Her hair was immediately in the way, flopping forward and grazing the keyboard. And probably in jeopardy of being obnoxiously in his face. She pushed it aside.

There, in scanned hand written scroll was her name: Élise Cantrelle. The document was some sort of tax form and she could clearly see the St. Philip address.

Head cocked to the side, Xavier was looking at her from the corners of his eyes. She couldn't quite read his expression, but God, she must totally be encroaching on his space.

"Sorry," she muttered, quickly backing away and removing her hand from his firm body.

He frowned and turned back to the screen. She decided to take a few steps back until she could no longer clearly see the computer, that way she wouldn't be tempted to get in his way. Not that she minded touching him or being close to him—quite the opposite—but he seemed a little annoyed by it.

"Okay, let's see what else we have..."

"Her husband was Nathanael," she said as he clicked away on the keyboard, pacing back and forth behind him. "He died of tuberculosis when she was pregnant with Amélie. Oh, she has three children—two boys and the little girl, Amélie. The boys are Jean-Michel and Matthieu. Amélie is three, Matthieu is six, and Jean-Michel is seven."

He glanced at her. "Were, you mean. They're dead now."

She stopped in her tracks. "Oh, right, of course." The idea of the children all dead made her heart ache. Of course they were dead, but she didn't like to think about it.

"I'm sorry. I didn't mean anything by it."

She forced a smile to replace the frown straining her lips. "I know. It's silly, but in my dreams they're very young. That's the only way I can envision them."

He studied her a few moments before returning his attention to the computer screen. He must think she was a real kook.

"Huh."

She didn't like the sound of that. "What's wrong?"

"Well, they're listed here as her children, but there no records of them after 1816, at least not in New Orleans."

"What does that mean?"

"They didn't get married, or buy a house, or own a business, or die for that matter, here."

"Where would they have gone?"

"You tell me."

"I don't know."

"Could they have moved?"

"I guess. Do you need that information?"

"It would help."

"Um…" She scanned through her memories— well, dreams—trying to find clues. There were none. On a whim, she suggested, "St. Louis?" It was where she'd been raised, and as far as she knew, her parents and grandparents.

She paced some more while he clicked away on the keyboard.

"St. Louis it is," he announced triumphantly. "Oh, that's horrible."

Not more bad news… "What?"

"Both Matthieu and Jean-Michel died in a house fire in 1820."

Her hand flew to her chest. "Oh my God. What about Amélie?"

"Let's see…" More clicks of the keyboard. "She apparently married in 1836 to Robert Dauger. They had one child, Gilles Dauger."

At that point the tracking seemed to get easier. A long line of only children and tragic accidents...the family tree never branched, leading straight to Lottie's mother and then, of course, to Lottie.

She stared unbelieving at the computer, her

heritage laid out before her. In many ways it was so disturbing to see such a direct path with absolutely no branches. How was that possible? How was it possible for her to be Élise's only descendant. Two hundred years and there was only her.

Xavier seemed at a loss for words as well. "Huh," was all he could utter.

"It's weird, right?"

"You could say that. You've had a rather unlucky family."

"Cursed is more like it. You know my parents died in a freak car accident. Single car accident, middle of the day, no ice, no rain, nothing. Just my parent's car and a tree. It was blamed on alcohol even though the toxicology reports came back inconclusive—whatever that means. My dad would have never driven drunk. I'd just gotten my permit and he was forever lecturing me about the dangers of drinking and driving, or texting and driving, or even talking to passengers. Besides, they barely ever drank and it was like, one p.m. on a Tuesday."

"That must have been horrible."

"It was even worse when the State couldn't find any family to take me. I was placed with complete strangers. There's something about shared blood that makes you feel less...alone. At least you have *something* in common with them."

Her eyes drifted to the computer. That long line of tragedy after tragedy twisting along the screen like an undulating snake. When did it end? When had it begun? Nathanael Cantrelle?

"What is she trying to tell me?" she muttered quietly. "Maybe she's trying to warn me...?"

"Lottie, wait. There could be a much simpler explanation."

"Like what?"

"Maybe it's all just repressed memories. You had a pretty tragic adolescence. Maybe coming to New Orleans simply triggered stories told to you when you were a kid."

"They're so real though."

"Your imagination could be filling in the details."

"Okay, I might be able to buy that, but what about the voices in my hotel room? And then when I saw Élise on the street, followed her and was shoved into traffic? What about the cemetery? I'm not suicidal. I didn't cut myself on purpose. I barely even remember doing it."

"You think the ghost of Élise Cantrelle did all those things?"

"Not all of them." She paced again in her small circle. "I can't imagine she would want to hurt me. But she's definitely trying to tell me something and I'm sure it has to do with the dreams."

"Like she can only communicate with you while you're asleep?"

"Yeah. But why not just come out and say what she wants?"

"I don't think it works that way. Communication between the living and dead is difficult, patchy. It usually has to come through images, pieces of memory, or just feelings."

She studied him, her eyebrows pushing tightly together. For someone who didn't believe her, he sure was helpful. And insightful.

"At least according to my mother," he added.

"But you don't believe any of it."

"Of course not."

She smiled inwardly. She wasn't so sure *she* believed that.

"Well, at least I know what I need to do."

"What's that?"

"I have to go back to sleep."

"You don't seem very tired to me. That might be a bit of a challenge."

"I have these pills. I kinda borrowed them from Amanda's stash."

His dark eyes narrowed. "What kind of pills?"

"Prescription sleeping pills. I haven't actually taken any," she lied. "I grabbed them just in case."

"You gotta be careful with that."

She was reminded immediately of Laurent when he'd warned Élise of the calomel. This wasn't the first time she'd seen Laurent in him. It was his eyes mostly, and his jaw and cheekbones, but even his mannerisms sometimes.

"I will," she reassured.

"There might be another way."

He said it almost...reluctantly, like he hadn't wanted to share. Maybe her intent to drug herself into sleep oblivion made him cave

"A séance. My mother hosts them all the time. I'm sure she'd be more than willing to help."

"Are you sure?"

"Oh yeah. She'd eat this shit—stuff—up."

"That sounds great. When do you think she could do it?"

"Well, no good séance happens during the day. It'll have to be tonight."

"I can't wait that long. Don't get me wrong, I still want to do it, but I need to find out what happens next. To Amélie, to Élise, with Laurent..."

"We know Amélie survives her fever."

"That's all we know."

"So you still plan on taking the sleeping pills."

"That or the old fashioned way—bourbon."

"I think bourbon might be the better choice."

She sighed when she realized what came next. "God, I really don't want to go back to the hotel and deal with Sam. Or even Amanda for that matter."

"Then don't. We have a guesthouse that's currently being remodeled. One of the rooms is finished. You're welcome to crash there."

"I don't get you. You don't believe any of this. In fact you seem to go out of your way to dissuade me, yet you keep offering help. Why?"

"I'm a man of mystery."

"More like mixed signals."

"Well, I don't blame you for not wanting to deal with Sam. I know I sure as hell wouldn't. And having you at the house will make it easier to coordinate with my scatter-brained mother. And maybe I feel a bit responsibility in all this."

"How?"

"This all started with my shop, my brother's tour."

"It started before that."

"Yeah but it definitely ramped up after. Now you're dreaming about my family...honor would demand I help you."

"Honor?" Snorting, she shook her head. "Whatever, I'll take it. And I appreciate it."

He bowed dramatically. "Any time, m'lady."

"Now you're just being a patronizing ass."

He grinned. "I am the master of mixed signals."

CHAPTER TEN

The Villere Guest House was tucked behind the main house, accessible through an alley closed off with an iron gate, and a brick courtyard filled with tropical plants. The two buildings formed an "L" shape, with a narrow wooden balcony lining the second story.

"There are four rooms in the Guest House," Xavier said. "Three are standard, hotel-type rooms and are all on the bottom level. The upper level is the suite and lucky for you, the one that's mostly finished." He wagged his eyebrows at her.

"Showering me with luxury, eh?"

"That's the way I roll." With a gentle placement of his hand on her shoulder, he nudged her toward the stairs. "There are actually two bedrooms in this unit. They've both been remodeled, as well as the en suites. The kitchenette and sitting room are another story."

He climbed the stairs and she followed a couple steps behind him. It was hard not to admire his physique. Broad shoulders that V'd down to a narrow waist and hips, and a well-shaped, muscular looking ass. In fact, his whole body looked well muscled. Through the thin fabric of his cotton Tee, she could

104

clearly see the curve of his lats and the deep valley where his spine rested between the bulk.

She could certainly imagine herself running her hand down that valley and testing whether or not his ass was as firm as it looked.

It was such a strange sensation—wanting to touch someone so much. She certainly wasn't a virgin by any stretch, but she never wanted to just grope a man. Granted, most the guys at her college were soft from drinking too much beer. In the body and the head.

He stopped at the door and turned to her. Afraid he'd caught her ogling, she quickly looked away. "The courtyard is really nice," she said by way of cover. "It's peaceful back here."

"Most of the time," he said as he placed the key—a normal key and not a hotel card—into the lock. "Until Grandmere has one of her late-night rituals, and then it's djembes and chanting and fire. It's like a Voodoo hippie drum circle."

She remembered the first memory Élise showed her of Sanite in the courtyard and was torn between shivering and laughing at the description.

"Will that be what it's like tonight?" she wondered as he opened the door.

"No. My mother will run the séance, so it'll be much weirder."

"Than a Voodoo hippie drum circle? I'm intrigued."

"You should be terrified of whatever craziness you're going to be subjected to. I know I am."

She gave him a hard look as she walked past him into the room. "You know, that's your family—and your heritage—you're making fun of. You should be more thankful."

"You're probably right. However, if you'd been

105

living with it for twenty-six years you might feel differently." He winked.

"Maybe."

Though outdated, the sitting room was nice enough. And clean, with a compact kitchen on the back wall—similar to the hotel suite she shared with Amanda and Sam. She could definitely see why they were in the process of remodeling. The couch and matching armchair were covered in a bold rose-covered fabric. It wouldn't have been bad if the pieces were remotely Victorian looking. They weren't. They were straight up from 1979. Add matching wallpaper and drapes and the room was almost nauseating to look at.

"Oh." She didn't mean to, but she cringed.

"Right? It's no wonder that in spite of our fabulous location and reasonable rates, occupancy at the Villere Guest House hasn't exactly been stellar. One of many changes I've implemented since taking over management. A website was the first change."

"There wasn't a website?"

"I'm not sure my mother or grandmother can even use a computer. Here. Check out the updated digs."

The bedrooms flanked the living area on either side. The one he led her to was a striking opposite to the design atrocity behind her. A huge, four-poster, dark mahogany bed dominated the room, draped in rich burgundy fabric that matched the window drapes. The only other piece of furniture was a matching wardrobe tucked into the corner and an ornate chair. They couldn't begin to take away from the bed's majesty. This room was made for one thing and one thing only. Well, two.

For some reason the thought made her blush. Probably because she immediately thought of the man beside her.

"Is that the bathroom?" She pushed past him to the open door of the en suite. All granite and claw-foot tub and the same mahogany wood around a large mirror.

"Well?"

She actually jumped at the sound of his voice. Just because she'd pictured him naked twice in the last ten minutes didn't mean she should turn into a nervous Nellie around him.

He was leaning against the doorjamb and watching her carefully.

"It's gorgeous. I love the historical feel."

"Thanks. I'm thinking this should help with business."

"Definitely."

He continued to stand there, trapping her in the bathroom. His eyes lingered on her and he looked like he wanted to say something. She wanted to ask, but her words were as trapped as his.

Finally, he pushed off the jamb. "Well, I guess I should let you try to get some shut-eye."

She could only nod and follow him back into the bedroom with the massive, gorgeous bed.

"Need anything?"

A couple silk scarves tying her wrists to one of those posts.

"Bourbon?" he prodded.

"I think I'm good. Thanks."

"I won't be far, so if you change your mind…"

It was possible she was imagining it, or hopelessly optimistic, but she thought she saw a glimmer of her own desires reflected in his dark brown eyes. He *was* lingering…

It didn't matter. This wasn't the time. She needed

to get back to Amélie and Élise and Laurent.

"I'll holler."

"Okay." He patted one of the bedposts, nodded tersely, and left.

Once alone, she sank wearily onto the mattress. What a mess. She was a mess. But she knew what she had to do. Fishing one of Amanda's pills from her purse, she swallowed it without water and settled back onto the plush mass of pillows, not bothering to get under the covers.

As she closed her eyes, a chill swept through the room and over her body. She ignored it, concentrating instead on the darkness of her eyelids. Amélie. Élise. Her family. The only family she had.

The darkness of her eyelids swirled around and around in her brain, quickly consuming her until she was back in the 19th century.

The longer Xavier stood outside the suite, the more he felt like a crazy stalker. First, he'd practically smothered her with his, "Need anything? You sure? Sure you don't need anything? I can get it for you." routine. Now, he was standing outside her window waiting for her to call for him or something?

It was pretty ridiculous.

Still, his feet didn't seem to be moving.

What *was* he waiting for?

The idea of her taking prescription sleeping pills bothered him. Especially since he was pretty sure the "grabbing them just in case" story was fabricated for his benefit. Not that he knew her in the least, but Lottie didn't seem like the type of girl who popped pills for fun. She *did* seem like the type of girl who would do what it took to get what she wanted or needed. And if that meant taking a double dose of sleeping pills to find out what her great-grandmother was up to, he was confident she wouldn't hesitate.

And that's how people OD'd.

But unless he wanted to sit by her bed and watch her sleep—which he kind of did, but not in a creepy way—there wasn't much he could do about it.

He waited for a ridiculous amount of time. Since he had a key, he *could* check on her. He could also knock on the door softly enough she wouldn't hear if she was sleeping. And what exactly would that prove? It would only tell him if she slept, not if she was lying in a pool of her own vomit because she'd taken too many sleeping pills.

He nearly bolted for the door at that thought but stopped himself. This level of worry was bordering on neurotic. He'd always been a worrier, he'd had to be. If it wasn't the fear his mother had left something on the oven, it was worrying whether or not Grandmere had taken her insulin.

Speaking of...

What a perfect distraction. Crossing the courtyard below, Grandmere walked with confident purpose. He called her name and jogged down to intercept her.

"Does the name, Élise Cantrelle, mean anything to you?" he asked when he reached her.

Recognition so brief it was barely a flicker crossed her wrinkled face. "No," she replied sharply and started walking again.

What the hell?

He jogged after her. For an old blind woman she moved awfully fast. Putting his body between her and whatever destination she was in such a hurry to get to, he placed a hand on her shoulder to stop her.

"Grandmere, are you lying to me?"

Her unseeing eyes glared at his hand. "Take your paws off me, child."

He dropped his hand but didn't move. "Élise Cantrelle? You know the name, don't you? Is she associated with Grandpere Laurent?"

"I don't know what you're talking about. Now, stand aside."

"No. You do know and you aren't telling me. Why?"

"There are some things you'd be best to forget. The name Élise Cantrelle is one. I know I never heard it." With a shove of her wrinkled arm, she pushed him aside and continued into the house.

He wasn't sure if the day could get any weirder and then he remembered the séance and realized it definitely would.

And that was a task he could do to keep his mind off Lottie. She probably didn't need him busting into her room like he was her keeper or some shit.

His mother was set up on Jackson Square reading fortunes. She not only loved the idea of a séance when he proposed the idea, she was ecstatic about it. Until she got sidetracked looking for her second deck of cards. Why she'd even been compelled to look for them he couldn't say, but took it as his cue to take off.

"So, we're on for ten p.m.?"

"Midnight would be better."

Of course, he thought sarcastically.

"I know." It took a bit of effort to keep his true feelings on the matter hidden from his tone. "But my friend is pretty anxious to contact her relative, so the earlier the better."

"Okay, but don't blame me if it doesn't go as well."

"I'm sure it'll be fine. You won't forget?"

"Please." Her brow furrowed. "God, where are those stupid cards?"

She was so focused on finding the missing deck she didn't notice him leave.

He popped into Central Grocery for a Muffaletta and then headed back to the Guest House. When there was no answer when he knocked softly on the suite door, he very carefully let himself in. The sitting room was quiet, the door to Lottie's room shut. After slipping the sandwich into the fridge he paused at the closed door, pressing his ear to the wood.

There was only silence on the other side. Of course that could be good or bad. He knocked gently. When there was no answer he cracked open the door. God, he felt like such a weirdo peering in on her, but if he didn't make sure she was okay he'd be a wreck all day.

Curled in a ball, she slept soundly on top of the comforter. Her breathing soft and steady and perfectly unalarming.

He quickly shut the door.

He'd put her number into his phone after sneaking it from Sam's contacts. Sending her a text requesting a reply the moment she woke, he left the suite and occupied himself in the store.

By the time the tour-group departed, she still hadn't responded. The store had been incredibly busy, so he'd been able to put it out of his mind. But once the shop was locked up, empty and quiet, anxiety sped through his veins. How many hours had she been asleep now?

Rushing back to the Guest House, he bolted up the stairs two at a time, and not so quietly let himself into the suite. He rapped hard on the door to her room.

"Lottie?" he called. Nothing. He knocked harder. "Lottie!" Still nothing.

"Fuck." He shoved open the door. So she'd looked like she was only sleeping earlier, he should have never left her alone.

She was still curled up on the bed, her blond hair fanning wildly on the pillow. Her face perfectly smooth, her expression blissfully peaceful. No vomit, blood, or any other leaked body fluids to make him panic.

He sat on the bed beside her. She didn't so much as stir. As knocked out as she was, there was no doubt in his mind she'd taken those pills.

"Lottie," he said, gently shaking her.

Nothing.

He shook her again. She whimpered but didn't rouse.

He shook her more firmly. "Lottie," he repeated.

She mumbled something he couldn't quite make out. Bending close to her face, he said her name again.

"Merci, mon hero, mon amour. Je suis eternellement reconaissant."

"Hey," he murmured, leaning close to her face. "Don't leave me hanging. I don't speak French. Wake up." He patted her cheek. "Please."

Her bright blue eyes fluttered open. "Xavier," she breathed and then completely took him by surprise by grabbing his head and pulling his lips to hers.

Her kiss was soft and sensual, yet intense. Hungry. So, so hungry. He welcomed the gentle thrust of her tongue as she pressed for more.

And he would love to give her more. As the kiss intensified and their positions changed so her back was pressed to the bed and he hovered above, he wondered how far it was going to go.

He wasn't quite prepared for it and he certainly hadn't expected it, but it wasn't like he hadn't thought about it. In fact, he'd spent a little time this morning thinking about it.

Her lips pulled away and he found the soft skin below her ear.

"Mon amour," she repeated. "J'ai besoin de toi."

He might not understand the words, but he certainly liked the sensual way they slid from her lips.

"Laurent," she moaned.

He stopped. Abruptly and without warning. She writhed under his grasp, rolling her body against his.

"Qu'est-ce qui ne vas pas?"

Oh shit. Was she still sleeping? Jerking back, he moved to sit on the edge of the bed.

She blinked a few times, rubbed her eyes, and then slowly, unsteadily rose. Perched on one hand, she rubbed her eyes again. She smiled when she saw him. "Hey," she said, her voice full of gravel. It sounded nothing like the sexual purr from moments earlier. There was no doubt in his mind she'd been asleep while kissing him.

"Hey," he said back, keeping his tone light, trying to cool the heat running through his body. "Thought I was going to have to get Prince Charming in here to wake you up."

Her smile was sly, like she was remembering something naughty. If she only knew...

She ran a hand through her wildly tousled hair. God, she looked so damn sexy with her bedroom hair, lidded eyes, lips pink and full from being kissed.

And happy. She looked so damn happy.

Too bad he wasn't the reason for her happiness. "So, what did you find out?"

"Oh my God, Xavier, it's so wonderful. Amélie is

fine. He healed her. Laurent healed her! By the next morning her fever was completely gone. And Élise...she was so happy she ran down to the French Market where Rosette said he often sells herbs and tinctures and medicines, and well..." She bit her lip. "They're having dinner tonight!"

The pure joy on her face, the beaming smile, the sparkle in her beautiful blue eyes, the story...it was so familiar. Too familiar. And now he knew why. In an instant he was pulled into the memory, the dream he'd had over and over for years. The dream he'd had again last night.

It always started the same, the woman he now knew to be Élise Cantrelle bounding toward him, Lottie's joyful smile lighting up her beautiful face, and throwing her arms around his neck.

"You did it!" she cried. "You cured her! She is perfect."

Though he knew he shouldn't, he couldn't help but return her embrace. The smell of roses drifted from her silky blond hair, and her soft body fit perfectly in his arms.

"I am so very happy for you."

Her arms still linked firmly around his neck, she pulled back to look at him. "There are no words. There is no amount of money that could repay you. There is no end to my thanks."

"This is all the payment I could ever need. Seeing your joy..." His words trailed off as his gaze lingered on hers. If he could only press his lips to hers, share her joy with the passion she stirred in him, love her as a man should love a woman.

But he couldn't. And they were in a public place.

She must have made the realization as he did, because she released him at the same moment he

114

released her and stepped back to an appropriate distance.

"Monsieur Villere," she said formally. "You must be willing to accept some payment..."

"We discussed this. I will not take a penny from you." The words sounded serious but his heart was not.

"Then dinner. I insist you have dinner at my home in lieu of payment. Tonight. Eight p.m. It would be very rude of you to refuse me." She gave him a cross look but her eyes still sparkled with overflowing joy.

He bowed his head. "I wouldn't dare insult you by refusing."

Her broad smile returned. "Perfect." She curtseyed. "I must go. My daughter..."

"Of course."

In the same bounding stride, she scampered away. Briefly she paused at a scowling American man and gave him a quick curtsey. "Henry." He heard her say. "I'm afraid I cannot stay." And then she was gone.

Turning back to the cart, a smile still pulling at the corner of his mouth, Sanite blocked his path, scowling.

"What are you doing with that white woman?" she hissed.

"Nothing."

"Nothing? Is that why she threw herself all over you?"

"She was merely overjoyed," he said dismissively. "I had the pleasure of tending to her sick child last night. The child is recovered."

"Overjoyed." Sanite snorted and shook her head. "I saw the way she looked at you, and you her. Everyone here saw it as well."

Laurent glanced around. "It appears no one cares but you."

"It's a bad idea and you know it. A white woman and a Creole of color..."

"This coming from a white man's mistress."

"It's different and you know it. You need to stay away from her."

"Your concern is duly noted. But not warranted. I have nothing but honorable intentions."

"The intentions of men may start honorable but never stay that way."

He swallowed his anger. "Your opinion has been heard, sister. You may now keep it to yourself."

"Xavier?" His name sounded almost foreign. Élise's—Lottie's—bright blue eyes were rimmed with concern. He wanted to take her in his arms as Laurent had held Élise. Only they weren't in public...

How hadn't he put the pieces together? Oh, that's right. Because it was impossible. He couldn't be dreaming a scene from the past, a scene from Laurent Villere's life. No more than Lottie could be dreaming the same scene from her own ancestor's path. That shit didn't happen.

"What's wrong?"

What's wrong...

He suddenly realized what she'd asked earlier when he'd pulled away. *Qu'est-ce qui ne vas pas...* "What's wrong" in French.

"Do you speak French?" he wondered.

"No."

"Me neither."

"My dreams have been in French though. Somehow I speak it then."

He realized his dream was also in French. It felt

116

like his native tongue, but if he thought hard enough, if he bothered to try to remember details, he could pull out phrases. Like, *J'ai besoin de toi*...I need you.

He cleared his throat. "Hey, are you hungry? I picked up a Muffaletta—the best in New Orleans."

"Starving."

"Perfect. Me too."

CHAPTER ELEVEN

Confused, Lottie watched him disappear from the room. It wasn't just his out of the blue questions or abrupt change in conversation that made her feel so disoriented. Her head was filled with Jell-O—even worse than earlier. And her limbs felt like they belonged to someone else. Attached to another body, in another time, another dimension.

Amanda's pills worked like a charm, maybe even too well. Someone may as well have unscrewed her head and put in on another body as disjointed as she felt.

Not only that, but her emotions were also a swirling mix of bewilderment. Residual elation from Élise seeped from her bones, conflicting with the sense of unease she'd been plagued with for the last several days. And waking up and seeing Xavier sitting on the bed hadn't put a damper on that elation. Even if he'd been a little weird, she still liked seeing him, being near him, touching him...

She had no idea how he felt about her. What did she call him earlier? The master of mixed signals? Was he there because he cared, because he was suspicious, because he enjoyed a good train-wreck...?

His head popped into the door.

"Food's up."

Commanding legs that didn't want to listen, she staggered into the other room, instantly nauseated by the affront of roses. She must have stumbled because Xavier rushed to her side and steadied her.

Putting a hand to her forehead to stop it from spinning, she offered a pathetic smile. "Sorry. I guess I slept too long."

He frowned. "Let's get you some fresh air." He eased her out the door on onto the balcony.

The sweet, thick, hot air didn't do much for her nausea, but being away from the rose invasion helped.

"There's a table in the courtyard," he offered, leading her across the balcony.

She balked when they reached the top of the stairs. "Just give me a second. I'll be fine in a little bit."

"You'll be better once you have a little food in you."

She let out a startled scream as he scooped her up and carried her down the stairs. She stared at him incredulously. "You're kidding me."

He grinned. "It's hot up there and I'm hungry. And you're making me nervous teetering around."

"You're carrying me to the table?" She couldn't quite believe the words even as they poured from her mouth.

"I haven't worked out yet today. I could use the exercise."

"Want to run me around the block then?"

"Maybe later when the evening cools off. You're light, but you're not *that* light." He set her in a wrought iron chair and dashed back up the stairs.

She was still musing about how he'd just carried down a flight of stairs when he returned with a large paper covered sandwich and two Barq's root beers. Spreading the paper on the table, he flipped a chair around and straddled it. Grabbing one half of the huge sandwich, he nodded toward the other. "Dig in."

With the first swallow of bread and meaty goodness on its way to her stomach she realized it was the first food her lips had touched that day. "This is good," she said.

"Hell yeah. Like I said, best in town."

She was so famished, she devoured the entire sandwich with barely a breath between swallows.

Xavier was grinning at her. He still had half of his sandwich. "Hungry?"

Her cheeks got decidedly warmer. "You could say that. Dreaming of ghosts takes a lot out of a girl."

His expression was unreadable as he took a gulp of root beer.

"You still don't believe me do you?"

"I don't know what I believe."

He might not know what to believe but she wasn't sure what to think. On one hand he seemed to support her unconditionally—the library, giving her a place to crash, suggesting the séance...

What was his motive? It wasn't like he was always hitting on her. There were times when it seemed like that could be the case, when he genuinely acted like he was into her. But other times, he looked at her like she was some sort of social experiment.

It was a look she was used to. Throughout high school as the kid without parents and then in college, as the girl who acted like a parent, she'd been a curiosity to those around her for the last eight years. Why should Xavier be any different?

Because she wanted him to be different. Because she wanted him to understand.

"So, what should I expect for the séance?"

Xavier finished the last bite of his sandwich, flipped his chair around, and then leaned back in it. "Well, it depends on whether my mother is in a Voodoo mood, or a Native American mood, or in fortune-teller mode."

"Such a collection."

"She's a little...well, different. Okay, a lot different."

"How so?"

His expression became exacerbated as he sucked in a breath of air and blew it out. "Besides seeing things that aren't there—"

"Like dead people?"

"Yeah."

"I can relate."

He quickly took another drink of root beer. Perhaps to hide his reaction.

"Go on," she encouraged, realizing she'd made him uncomfortable.

He offered a pained smile. "Let's just say I'm surprised when she remembers to put pants on in the morning."

"Ah."

"It certainly made for an interesting childhood. Especially after my dad bailed and Grandpere died. Grandmere is a tough old lady, but being blind and diabetic, she's not exactly in a place to run a household. And Julien might be the eldest, but he was more interested in partying with his friends than making sure the electric bill got paid."

"So that responsibility fell on you?"

"Yeah."

"How old were you?"

"Thirteen."

She smiled sadly. "I was fifteen when my parents died. It's a tough way to grow up."

"Like being thrown to the wolves."

"Wearing a belt made of bacon."

"Or a suit." He grinned. "Oh, that cliché never gets old."

"When it's appropriate..." She shrugged. "So that must have been tough—assuming adult responsibilities at such a young age."

It was his turn to shrug. "It suits my personality. Even when I was little, I spent way too much time worrying about other people. Had Grandmere taken her insulin, should Grandpere be smoking so much, did my dad get home safely from a night at the bars...? It drives me crazy. I can only imagine how nuts it makes those around me."

"You care. That's what's important."

"What about you? I can't begin to understand what you went through being orphaned at fifteen. I might not be able to get away from my family, but I certainly wouldn't want to be without them."

"Being in the *system,* I didn't have the responsibilities you did. For the most part, things were taken care of. But I continually watched my foster siblings self-destruct. I nearly followed the same path. It just made me really aware of those tendencies and how important it is that I avoid them."

"Hence Sam's *fun-sponge* comment."

"You heard that? I was hoping you hadn't."

"Well, I certainly didn't think anything of it, other than Sam is a bitch."

She couldn't help the laugh that erupted through her closed lips. She quickly wiped her face.

"Sometimes..."

"Why do you associate with her?"

"Amanda." Guilt washed through her as she realized she hadn't contacted her friends. They had no idea where she was or what she was doing. She made a mental note to send them a text later. "We roomed together in the dorms for several years and became pretty close. She and Sam are childhood friends. We never hit it off, but Sam tolerates me because of Amanda and vice-versa. We usually get along okay, but sometimes Sam just seems to have it out for me. Usually when she's drunk."

"Probably because you represent everything she wants to be but can't."

"A fun-sponge?"

"In control. Responsible."

Lottie nodded. "A fun-sponge."

They were suddenly sitting close enough together that he was able to nudge her shoulder with his. She wasn't sure when they'd migrated to such close proximity, or how it had even happened, but they had, and suddenly she was *too* aware of it.

His gaze caught hers and she froze. Her heart immediately jumped into overdrive, pounding a ferocious techno beat in her chest. His beautiful brown eyes—Laurent's eyes—slowly drifted down her face until they lingered on her mouth.

Her lungs seized. He was going to kiss her. Swallowing, she leaned forward, ready to meet him, ready to taste the sweetness of his kiss, when a strong gust of wind abruptly blew through the courtyard, sending their trash scattering and knocking over the half-full bottles of Barq's, sending root beer everywhere.

They both jumped up to avoid being soaked,

although it was too late for Lottie. Covered in the sticky liquid, she righted the bottles, while Xavier retrieved the trash.

"That was weird," he said when he returned. He took the empty bottles from here. "Let me throw these away. Man, it really got you."

"Yeah. I could probably use a shower and fresh change of clothes. I hate to go back to the hotel though. I really don't want to deal with Sam, or Amanda, for that matter."

"Don't. Use the Guest House shower. They've been remodeled, remember?" He winked. "As far as the clothes, we can wash those. I have shorts and a Tee you can borrow."

There he was being super helpful again. But hadn't he said that was his personality? Maybe it had nothing to do with her after all.

"Are you sure?"

"Of course. Séance should be ready in an hour or so. Just let me grab some toiletries and towels and fresh clothes, you can take a shower, and we'll be ready to roll."

It was amazing how easily he skipped over their near kiss, over everything. He just dismissed it like it was no big deal, like nothing was a big deal, including her.

"Okay, thanks."

"No problem. Head up to the room, I'll be right up with your stuff."

She gestured toward the trash in his hand. "Want me to throw that stuff away?"

"I got it." And with that he zipped from the courtyard.

Exasperated, she ran her hands through over her face and through her hair. Well, at least the control of her body had returned to her, she thought as she climbed the stairs up to the suite. It was the only thing that was normal.

As promised, within minutes, Xavier brought some fluffy white hotel towels, tiny bottles of shampoo, conditioner, lotion, a mini bar of soap, fresh bandages, and a T-shirt and athletic shorts—both with Tulane blazoned on them. As quickly as he arrived, he dipped back out of the room. It was like he was suddenly the hotel manager tending to a guest and not her...

It made no sense she should care. Why should she be anything to him? After all, he was a stranger. A man she was bothering with her idiotic ghost sightings. Nothing more. Nothing less.

With a sigh, she stripped down and stepped into the shower. There was no point worrying about it now. She had more pressing concerns. The ghost sightings weren't idiotic, she knew that. Élise Cantrelle—her great-great grandmother, the only relative she had at the moment—was trying to communicate with her. And Lottie had no doubt it was something important. She had every intention of listening.

Which is why when the sound of her name seeped in with the water droplets, instead of giving into the fear creeping through her tissues, she stood completely still and strained her ears.

The sound of her name slowly gained strength, getting louder and louder.

"I'm here," she said finally, her voice sounding desperate. "I hear you. Tell me what you need."

It took a moment, but finally the voice responded, strained at first, weak even. "C'est dangereaux," it—

she—said.

"I don't speak—"

"Vous êtes en danger."

She tried to commit the foreign words to memory. "Please…"

"S'il vous plait!"

The voice echoed Lottie's plea. It was the one French phrase she knew.

"Fais attention!"

"QUITTEZ!" Another voice—stronger, angrier—assaulted her from every angle, just as the water went from warm to scalding hot.

She screamed, struggling to get out from under the shower spray. Fumbling with the handle, she somehow managed to turn the water "up" instead of "off", sending liquid acid pouring down her back. She screamed again, returning to the tap with shaking hands and successfully stopping the flow of lava this time.

Body heaving, skin burning, she stood in the shower for a long time, dripping and in a state of shock.

What was that? It wasn't—couldn't have been Élise. The feel…the presence was all wrong. The first voice had been desperate, pleading. The second…hateful. Were there two ghosts?

Whatever fear she'd been able to suppress assaulted her with a vengeance. With trembling hands, she gingerly wrapped one of Xavier's fluffy towels around her stinging skin. She didn't bother drying her hair and it clung to her scalp, dripping down her back and over her shoulder.

The bathroom no longer felt safe. That had been the third time something weird had happened in the bathroom and she was beginning to think it was somehow tied to running water. Whatever it was, she was ready to get the hell away from it.

Unfortunately, the bedroom wasn't any safer. Standing with his back to her, staring at something in his hands, was Julien.

She froze. Unsure what to do. Afraid to make a noise. Should she run back into the bathroom? Lock herself in with whatever ghost hated her? Or did she bolt for the door? Escape to the courtyard.

She wasn't sure why Julien suddenly frightened her. It wasn't like he'd ever really done anything *to* her, but something felt off. The energy in the room was sinister. It shared the same unmistakable anger the second ghost had vehemently showered over her.

He turned. In his hands were Xavier's T-shirt and shorts.

"Ah, look who it is. The cutter." He held up the clothes. "I see my brother is taken with you."

"I spilled root beer—"

"Oh, I'm sure. A very convenient ruse." Still clutching the clothing, his hand flew to his forehead in a mocking *fainting* gesture. "Oh my!" he exclaimed in a high-pitched voice. "I'm just soooo clumsy. Spilling this soda all over me." His hands traced feminine curves down his torso. "Whatever will I do?"

She stared at him. He was nuts. That's all there was to it.

Vile hatred suddenly washed over his face and he threw the clothes at her. Clutching her towel with one hand, she attempted to catch the clothing with the other. She managed to grab the T-shirt but the shorts fluttered to the floor.

Julien was suddenly inches from her, his eyes filled with so much anger, the whites were barely visible. She'd seen those eyes before. In the courtyard.

127

On Sanite Villere.

"I won't let you take advantage of his generosity. I won't let you manipulate his good will."

She swallowed. She wanted to retort. She needed to punch him in the face, but she was frozen by his putrid energy.

"What the hell?" Xavier rushed over, placing his body slightly in front of her, like he was shielding her from Julien. "What are you doing here?" he asked his brother.

Julien stepped back, holding up his hands like he was surrendering. The anger was suddenly wiped clean from his handsome face. "I heard a scream. I came to investigate. How was I supposed to know you were using the Guest House to entertain *friends*..."

"Shouldn't you be knee-deep in your tour?"

Parking his ass on the bed, Julien shrugged. "Ended early."

She couldn't see Xavier's face, but the way he shook his head told her he thought Julien's answers sounds like a bunch of bullshit. She agreed.

He turned to her, concern straining his features. "Are you okay?"

His body blocked her from Julien's view. She shook her head.

Xavier immediately turned back to his brother. "Why don't you get out."

"Oh little brother, you're such a tease."

"I'm not kidding. Get the fuck out."

With a shrug of his shoulders, Julien rose. "See ya around," he said to her. It felt like a threat.

She didn't relax until she heard the hotel door open then shut. She let out a shuddering sigh.

"My God, Lottie, what happened?"

Acutely aware she wore only a towel and

clutching the fabric close with one hand, she shook her head. "You won't believe me."

"Tell me anyway."

"I was taking a shower—obviously—and I started hearing voices. Well one voice, at first. Élise, I'm sure. And she was talking to me in French, begging me to do…something. Then another voice interjected, screamed at me really. And then the water suddenly got really hot. I'm sure someone just flushed a toilet in the house or something."

"The rooms are on a separate system than the house," he said quietly.

"In one of the other rooms?"

"Maybe…"

"I think there might be two ghosts. Élise and one that's trying to hurt me. God, what do you think?"

He frowned. Again. He frowned a lot.

"Oh right, you don't think there are ghosts at all."

He ran his hand over the back of his neck. "Lottie, I—"

"Just go in the other room so I can change. Please."

He pursed his lips like he was trying to keep words from escaping, nodded tersely, and slipped from the bedroom.

She waited for the click of the latch before releasing the towel. Even then she hustled to dress. Luckily, her panties had escaped the root beer soaking—she would have felt weird going commando in his shorts. Her bra wasn't so lucky. She was of medium bustiness, so enough to be noticeable, but not so much to be obscene.

It wasn't until she was fully clothed that she could think about things. She quickly decided she didn't want to think about it. It was all too much. And adding Xavier's reluctance to believe anything she said, in spite of his unwaveringly support, just poured salt into the gaping wound.

Speaking of...

The red line on her wrist stared at her angrily. Shit, the bandages were in the bathroom. With a grimace, she dashed into the room, yanked them off the vanity and dashed back out. Covering the cut let her pretend it wasn't there, which was exactly what she needed.

After taking enough deep breaths she might as well have been in a Yoga class, and attempting to dismiss every strange thing that had happened, she opened the bedroom door.

Xavier was sitting on the arm of the rose bomb explosion couch and jumped up the moment the door opened. Jesus, what was she supposed to make of that? He was so anxious about her arrival he was sitting on the edge of the couch—literally—but yet he didn't believe a word of the biggest mystery of her life.

Talk about a mind fuck.

She couldn't worry about that now. She needed— wanted—his support. In reality, she'd take it anyway she could get it.

"Do you want a drink?" he asked. "Like a cocktail, not a root beer."

Normally, she'd hesitate drinking a cocktail just to relax. It only led down a bad path. Normally.

"Yes. Man...Yes." She let out a pent up breath. "That sounds amazing."

The pleasure on his face was almost sexual as he retrieved a growler and two pint classes from the end table. He must have brought them up with him. "You like beer, right?"

"I like whatever you're serving."

For the next thirty minutes, they sat on the balcony and shared the growler, talking about anything and everything that didn't include ghosts or séances or weirdness in general—which suited Lottie just fine. They talked about school and their chosen degrees. She learned that while Xavier was dismissive of his family legacy, he still wanted to preserve it, and had pursued a business degree with a minor in hotel management in order to make sure the Villere household could remain in its historical home.

He seemed particularly interested in her history and especially what life was like growing up in foster care. Apparently after his dad left (not a Villere. Xavier assumed his mother's name when his dad abandoned them), he and Julien were nearly taken from the home by social services—all because Julien had skipped so much school the authorities were alerted. When they came to investigate, there was no electricity or water in the house. By some stroke of luck, the social workers dropped the case less than twenty-four hours after the notice was given. They never came back. Never followed up. They pretty much disappeared.

She didn't mind talking about foster care life. After all, she had every intention of talking about it daily for the rest of her life. It hadn't been an easy journey, but if she could help one kid deal with their situation or even make it better, it would all be worth it.

The growler drained, relaxed from the alcohol, she felt content. The heat of the day had finally dissipated, and the night air was cool against her scalded skin. Sitting with Xavier felt natural, good.

She heard him sigh and at first thought they

might be sharing a sentiment. But it wasn't a content sigh. "Shit, we have about ten minutes before the séance." He turned to her. "Are you ready for this?"

"Not at all."

"Good." He rose and offered his hand. She gladly took it and he pulled her to her feet. "That makes two of   us."

CHAPTER TWELVE

Lottie's hand was once again captured by Xavier's warm firm grip as he led her through the interior of the house and into a dark room closed off by large wooden French doors. The gesture was reassuring more than intimate, but she was grateful for his touch, no matter the intent.

Although they might have just been heavily draped, there were no visible windows in the room. But differentiating a window dressing from the yards of fabric adorning the walls would be an impossible task. All that cloth made the room feel closed in and somewhat creepy, which was probably the point. A curving mahogany staircase leading up to more darkness sat on the opposite wall.

The room may have once been used for dining, but she doubted anyone ate in it any more even though there *was* a round wooden table in the center of the room, and a buffet on the wall closest to her.

A woman in her early fifties—presumably Xavier's mother—with long, wild, curly black hair sat in the chair facing them. Her eyes were closed, hands outstretched palm up and resting on the table. Her lips moved silently.

Before her were a bowl of sand and three unlit pillar candles surrounding a tall, wooden structure. To Lottie's untrained eye, it looked like an animal head totem pole. A single dim light hung from an antique fixture directly above the table, a pair of shriveled up bird talons dangling from it. The room smelled strongly of herbs and earth.

Releasing her hand after giving it a final squeeze, Xavier pulled out a chair and pushed gently across her back, encouraging her to take a seat. He took the chair to her left.

She inhaled deeply in an attempt to calm her chattering heart. She wanted to be here. She wanted answers. But having no idea what to expect made her stomach flutter with anxiety.

Once they were seated, his mother opened her eyes—dark eyes like Xavier and...Laurent. Her smile revealed bright white teeth behind deep red lipstick. "Good evening. I'm Delia Villere. Charlotte correct?"

"Most people call me Lottie."

"Lottie..." Delia made a face. She must not like the nickname. "Hmm. Lottie..." She ran a finger through the sand. "Lottie..." She lit the three candles. "Tell me Lottie, do you see the head of the deer on the energy totem?" She gestured toward the sculpture at the center of the table. Lottie nodded. "The deer is your spirit animal, showing your compassion, gracefulness, femininity, and lust for adventure. She will guide you tonight and protect your spirit from harm." Closing her eyes, she began to chant low, guttural words.

After at least a minute of chanting, her eyes flicked open and focused on Xavier. "And you," she said. "The cougar is your spirit animal. He is one of great leadership, loyalty, courage, responsibility, and foresight. He will guide you and protect you from harm."

Lottie was pretty sure she saw Xavier roll his eyes.

Delia turned back to her. "My Xavier tells me you wish to channel the spirit of a dead relative."

"Yes, my—"

Delia held up her hand. "Don't tell me," she said, closing her eyes again. "It's a distant relative. One you were once close to but something happened. Something—"

"Jesus Christ, mom," Xavier interjected, the irritation evident in his voice. "Skip the dog and pony show. Élise Cantrelle. We want to contact the spirit of Élise Cantrelle."

The light above the table flickered.

Delia made another face and Lottie found herself following the older woman's lead. She gave Xavier a *look*.

One he definitely noticed. "Sorry," he mouthed. "Mom," he said with a much softer tone. "Doesn't it help to know who you're trying to contact?"

"Of course."

Xavier's brow scrunched together for a brief second, but didn't say anything. Until she started using the sand to draw a symbol on the table.

"No, mom. That won't work. This spirit is probably earthbound."

Delia stared at him. Lottie stared at him.

He held up his hands. "I mean, I assume. *She's* contacting you, right? In your dreams?"

Lottie nodded, still staring at him in shock. Didn't he say he didn't believe any of this?

"Élise is speaking to Lottie in her dreams," he

explained to Delia. "Doesn't that mean she's earthbound?"

"It does. Without Papa Legba to open the gate, spirits inside Guinee cannot normally contact the outside world. Unless they are very strong..." Delia still seemed confused and shocked as she explained what Xavier already seemed to know.

Lottie could relate. She was officially, positively confused. And not just by Xavier's behavior.

"Well, that changes things." Delia moved the bowl of sand aside. "We will need to join hands."

Delia's small, cool hand was such a contrast to Xavier's. Lottie glanced at him and without turning his head, he caught her gaze from the corner of his eyes.

Ready, he mouthed, his eyebrows bobbing once as he squeezed her hand.

She started to reply when Delia's instructions cut her short.

"Close your eyes," she said, a little sternness to her voice, like she knew they weren't paying attention. "We need to concentrate on the spirit. Concentrate on the memory of Élise Cantrelle."

The light flickered again. Okay, that was the second time it had done that. Lottie really wanted to watch to see if it happened again, but decided she should probably follow Delia's instructions if she hoped for this séance to be successful.

Reluctantly, she obeyed. Clamping her eyes shut, she tried to focus entirely on Élise. It wasn't so easy with Xavier's hand wrapped around hers but with effort, she managed to shut out all distractions, including him.

"We are trying to contact the spirit of Élise Cantrelle," Delia called in a powerful voice. "Mother, grandmother, lost spirit... Can you hear us?"

Nothing. The light may have surged again, but since her eyes were closed, Lottie couldn't be sure.

"Élise Cantrelle," Delia called again, louder, more powerfully.

The light definitely surged again, she was sure of it this time. The reds of her lids glowed from the quick flash of brightness.

"Will you respond to us? Your granddaughter of ten generations, Lottie, and Xavier Villere, descendant of great and powerful Voodoo mothers and fathers."

A low vibration buzzed through the room, mildly rocking the table back and forth.

"Use our energy, spirit of Élise Cantrelle. Focus on the desire of your blood to bring you to this place, to us."

The table began to rock so violently the totem came crashing down. Lottie let out a startled scream as she jumped back, releasing both Delia and Xavier's hands. She jerked her face left to see Xavier watching the fallen totem like he was hypnotized. Following his gaze, she gasped out loud when she saw the deer's eyes freakishly shifting from person to person and then finally locking with hers. She held its stare, unable to move. Frozen. Exactly how Xavier had been.

She knew her eyes were open, but also knew she was entering another time and place. Stripped of their fabric coverings, the walls seemed to drip away years of paint and wallpaper. Her peripheral vision suddenly ceased when the tunnel she entered whizzed by with images and smells.

A man hovered above her, his eyes filled with desire. Desire she could feel in her bones.

"Tu es trop belle."

She knew exactly what he said. "You are too

beautiful."

His lips were so full, so luscious...And covered hers in the most amazing, delectable kiss she had ever felt, quickly becoming deeper, more passionate, with more purpose, more drive.

She didn't feel like herself. She wasn't herself. Her body no longer under her control. She only knew that she had an equal amount of passion and desire for this man. The emotions were too intense to ignore. She became lost in it...torn from one world to the next. It was impossible, yet utterly fulfilling at the same moment and she succumbed to it, disappearing into the glorious, all-encompassing sensation of his lips on hers.

Too soon, though, she heard a voice. A voice filled with hate and torment. While her body continued to burn with lust and want, the voice grew louder.

"You will never set her free. Jamais. JAMAIS!"

In an instant the loud, terrible woman's voice was gone. Its echo rang through her ears long after it had vanished, even as the memory swarmed her.

Élise glanced at the clock for the hundredth time. Laurent would be arriving any moment now. Nervousness knotted her stomach as she dashed around the room, inspecting Rosette's handy work. Her finest china and silverware were displayed with precision. Prisms from the crystal wine goblets danced across the wall. Perfect.

She felt like she was forgetting something, though. Something important.

"Rosette!"

The maid peeked around the kitchen door. "Yes, Madame?"

"When, Monsieur Villere arrives, please escort him here. I will be back shortly."

Hitching the front of her dress, she climbed the stairs to the second floor bedrooms. Amélie was peacefully sleeping. Her transformation from one day to the next was nothing short of astounding. The danger had passed. She was going to live.

The relief Élise felt was overwhelming as she silently thanked the Holy Father. Laurent Villere did what no doctor was able to do, and her gratitude went beyond just dinner. She would have gladly paid him for his services. Money was precious but she would have surrendered any amount. That he was so kind to accept a mere dinner invitation said everything about his character.

She kissed her daughter's cool cheek and pulled up the blanket, tucking it on both sides. She paused at the door, waiting for the rambunctious murmurings of two little boys. Stillness. They were already asleep in the adjacent bedroom. Taking a deep breath she smiled and strolled back down the staircase.

There was still something amiss, but she couldn't begin to identify it.

Rosette met her at the landing. "Monsieur Villere is here," she said in a hushed voice. A grin tugged at the corner of her full lips. "I will fetch the wine."

"Thank you."

Rosette disappeared into the kitchen and Élise did everything in her power to calm her nerves. Dinner. It was only dinner. With an amazing, beautiful man...

Clearing her throat, she crossed the sitting room. The fine chiffon of her crimson dress floated behind

139

her as she walked, and she was very aware of the way it clung to her shape as she stepped into the dining room.

Laurent stood at the opposite wall, gazing thoughtfully at the painting of her family's Saumur estate hanging above the mantle. He was quite a sight to behold, his tall form commanding, his silk frock coat draped beautifully over broad shoulders that tapered to a perfectly trim waist. The soft light from the few candles topping the table illuminated his strong cheekbones, enhancing the raw masculinity of his face.

His dark eyes shifted to her and he took her in from head to toe before seeming to remember his manners and bowing. She would not deny she liked his obvious approval of her appearance.

"Good evening," he said.

She curtseyed, repeating the greeting.

He glanced around the room. "Will it only be the two of us for dinner?"

"Yes. I hope you do not mind the casual nature of my invitation."

"Not at all. I much prefer it."

The implications of their intimate dining situation were not unknown to her. And as his dark eyes lingered on her, she felt a blush burn her cheeks, as though she had already drank several glasses of wine.

Rosette darted in the room carrying the wine decanter and bowls of soup. Élise suffered a moment of guilt that Rosette was forced to balance so many items at once. If she had a proper serving staff it wouldn't be necessary. The servant handled it beautifully though, and with perfect grace she'd ladled the soup and poured the wine.

And suddenly Élise remembered what she was

forgetting. Henry's dinner invitation. It was too late to decline, but perhaps, if the moment presented itself, she could have Rosette deliver a note of regret to Henry's estate. Lying might be a sin, but she would still use Amélie's health as an excuse.

She swallowed, pushing the lapse in bad manners behind her. "Shall we sit, Monsieur Villere?"

He moved to prepare her chair. "Given the casual nature of our evening," he said as she took her seat. "I would ask you call me Laurent."

She adjusted the napkin in her lap. "If that is what you wish, Laurent. I would request the same."

"I am more than happy to fulfill any of your desires," he said as he bowed his head. His eyes flick up to meet hers. "Élise."

The sound of her name as it slid from his mouth flashed goose bumps over her skin and sent heat to the deepest recesses of her body. She quickly turned her attention to the soup, lest her nerves overwhelm her.

This was the first time she had been in the presence of a man who stirred her with such desire. She had loved her late husband. He was a gentle man with a mostly kind hand. A fortunate mix when so many other marriage arrangements fell short of love or kindness.

But what Laurent ignited within her was different. She couldn't deny the ache she felt for him, and knew it would be easy to lose herself in his eyes, his lips, his hands.

His decorum was perfect and they spoke only polite conversation during the main courses of dinner—of business and weather and the recent expansion of their city. The wine flowed freely and she did not hesitate to send Rosette for another carafe when theirs was empty.

141

"Dinner was wonderful," Laurent said at the end of the final course as Rosette placed bowls of sweet pudding before them. "I could not ask for a more delicious meal or dinner companion."

"It is the very least I could do for what you have done for Amélie."

"She is still well?"

"Yes. It's remarkable. A miracle really. It's like she was never sick." Élise looked down to hide tears suddenly gathering in her eyes. "I'm sorry," she said, discretely wiping them with the napkin. "Almost losing her was overwhelming."

Laurent's fingers softly touched her cheek and delicately brushed a tear away. "You need not apologize," he said. His fingers lingered on her face a moment longer before he pulled them away.

She very much wanted to receive his touch again.

"I understand. I have a young son myself. I fear his health is even more precious to me after his mother died during his birth."

"I am sorry to hear that." She shook her head. "It is hard to be widowed so early in life. My late husband died before Amélie was born. Tuberculosis. He was a strong, young man. It was shocking."

"Do you miss being married?"

It should have been an inappropriate question, but she felt comfortable sharing such a personal matter with him. "I am lucky my husband left me with a healthy estate and I am well taken care of. But... there are many things about married life I miss. Things money cannot buy."

"It can be very lonely," he agreed.

The wine was making her bold. "But you are a man. Surely you have your share of mistresses..."

"Not at all. I have been mostly content being a

celibate man. It wasn't until..." His gaze drifted over
her face. Abruptly, he cleared his throat. "I
apologize."

She ignored the dismissal. "Until what?" her
voice sounded two octaves too low.

His gaze lingered on her face, his dark eyes filled
with longing. "Until I saw you walking in the rain," he
finally replied in a quiet voice. "I cannot lie...I have
not stopped thinking about you since that moment."

She had no words. Desire had them trapped in
her throat. Her mouth opened, but only a stuttering,
"I...I..." came out.

With little warning, he leaned across the table
and kissed her. Startled at first, she hesitated. The
overwhelming sensation of his lips gently moving
against hers quickly shoved doubt and propriety
aside. She wanted more, needed more. She moved her
body closer to him.

His hand cupped her face and the kiss deepened.
Warm desire flooded her body and a murmur of
approval tickled her throat. Her lips parted and his
tongue touched hers with perfection. Purposeful yet
filled with passion and tenderness.

It was too much. Breaking the kiss, she stood
abruptly, panting for air. It went against everything
she'd ever been taught. It was wrong. It was
forbidden. Yet, how she wanted him...needed him...it
was as strong as the desire to breathe.

He rose as well. "I am sorry. I forget myself.
Please forgive me."

Élise lost what little bit of control made her pull
away. Her thoughts were devoured with torment while
her body ached with desire only his touch could
satisfy.

She reached for him, using the lapels of his coat

to pull him close, causing their hungry lips to crash together with force and determination.

The kiss was all consuming. Lust made her knees weak, causing her to stagger. Laurent broke the embrace long enough to scoop her into his arms. His lips covered hers again and she wrapped her arms around his neck.

A heat she'd never known burned through her body. It made her ache with desire. Desire that could only be fulfilled one way. Desire that could not be denied because of decency or what might be considered proper. *At that moment, she needed him more than anything, even more than decorum, especially more than decorum.*

"My boudoir," she murmured between kisses, "is across the hall from Amélie's room."

Closing her eyes, she hugged his neck tightly as he scaled the stairs, nestling into his neck, drowning in his scent, in the sensation of his hands on her flesh. She kept her hold firm until she heard the door quietly close behind them.

The second her feet hit the ground her eyes opened to his, filled with aching desire. Their hands began unbuttoning, pulling, and tugging at clothes. His coat, vest, shirt, her gown, and his trousers fell to a pile on the floor.

As the last string of her short corset was unlaced, he began feverishly kissing her jaw, her neck, the tops of her breasts.

"I am forever lost," he murmured.

She let out an approving moan to encourage him to keep going. He assisted her escape of her undergarments, following with kisses as she stepped away from her falling chemise. He once again scooped her into his arms and set her gently on the bed.

They were both fully unclothed and she couldn't avert her eyes from his bare chest, broad and muscular, tightening as he held his body above her. His gaze drifted over her body, lingering on her breasts and her lips, before settling on her eyes.

"You are too beautiful," he said, bending for another kiss.

She arched her back with anticipation, easing her legs apart, yearning for more of him. His kisses moved downward. Her nipples tightened and he rolled his tongue over the tips. His fingers trailed down her stomach and over her hips.

With quick breaths she pulled his head back to her lips. She needed him, his tongue in her mouth as his hand slipped between her legs. Sweet fire shot through her. She opened more for him, arching for more. "Mon Dieu," she moaned.

The first thrust when he entered her was euphoric. The second...ecstasy. It was as if her world had stopped and all she could see, feel and taste was him. Their bodies moved in perfect motion, pleasure shooting through her with each delectable thrust. His smell, his gentleness, his essence overwhelmed her.

He caught her eyes in a final lustful gaze when her body exploded into spasms of pure pleasure. Frantically trying to catch her breath she crumbled in his arms, just before he crumbled into hers.

CHAPTER THIRTEEN

In an instant, Lottie was torn from the memory. She blinked in the dim light, trying to regain her senses. Panting, her body burned with a passion that wasn't hers but felt just real, just as intense as if she'd actually been there, under Laurent, his lips on hers, his body heavy above her...

Cool liquid ran over her forehead and dripped down her cheek. Glancing up, she saw Delia sponging water from a pail onto her face. Across the room, Xavier was draped in his chair, an old woman with long, gray dreads mimicking his mother's action.

His chest rose and fell rapidly, and his skin glistened with a fine sheen of sweat. Everything about their conditions matched, down to the expressions of shock. His eyes lifted to meet hers and once there, held her gaze firmly.

She knew immediately.

Pushing Delia away and rising roughly to her feet, she clomped over to him with staggering steps. The old woman tending to him faced the other way and for a minute, Lottie was worried she was going to run into her. Somehow—perhaps because her

146

uncoordinated footsteps sounded like a herd of charging horses—the old woman moved aside just at the last moment, and Lottie collapsed to her knees on the carpet beside Xavier, clutching the arm of the chair for support. He tried to rise, but like her, his body was a clunky, slowly responding machine.

"You experienced it too," she panted.

His brows pushed together and he tried to shake his head, but she could see it in his eyes.

"You did. I know you did."

"I—"

She didn't let him finish. She couldn't let him keep lying to himself, to her. Grabbing his head, she pressed her lips to his, enveloping him in the most passionate kiss of her life. Letting every ounce of desire buzzing through her body pour into him with every thrust of her tongue. His response was no less passionate. Wrapping his fingers in her hair he locked her to him, seeming to devour every drop of her kiss.

It was only reluctantly that she finally pulled away. This was a passion unwilling to be sated with just a kiss and there were two unwelcome observers in the room.

"See," she whispered smugly. "You can't deny that passion. You can't deny you didn't live it."

"Is that why you kissed me?" He sounded appalled. "To prove to me I shared your vision?"

"Yes! See, you did! Laurent...Élise..." She shook her head. "The love between them... I couldn't let you deny it. And it's still in me, just like it's still in you. I can feel it. I know you do too."

"I was kissing you, Charlotte, not Élise Cantrelle."

"How do you—"

The most horrifying shriek interrupted her. She

turned to see the old woman looming ominously above them. Her eyes were clouded over, so white they were opaque. And wild. They were positively wild. Or maybe it was the halo of gray dreads.

Lottie was suddenly very frightened.

"Boy, I told you to forget that name!" She turned to Xavier's mother, who cowered under her stare. "And you!" The mother cowered even more. "You allowed this?"

"I don't...I don't know what—"

"Élise Cantrelle," the old woman shouted. The room seemed to shake with her anger. "Is that who you channeled? Élise Cantrelle?"

"Yes," Xavier's mom said meekly.

"You idiot. You fool! She will be so angry." The old woman charged toward Lottie, who cowered just like Delia. "You. Out." A plump, wrinkled arm reached for her, probably ready to drag her from the room. How those blind eyes could see her so accurately...

"Grandmere," Xavier said sternly, reaching across her to block the old woman's hand. "Lottie is here at my request."

"I don't care. She ain't welcome."

Not quite the hospitable reception she would have expected from an old lady.

"Grandmere! What has gotten into you?"

"Tell me Xavier, why did you attempt to contact Élise Cantrelle? Because of this girl? Is that why you even asked about her earlier?"

"It doesn't matter."

"It does, boy!" Grandmere turned her blind gaze back to Lottie. "I got nothin' against you personally, little girl, but that won't help anything. You need to leave this house. Now." Setting her round jaw, she

148

"hmphed", and walked from the room.

Lottie stared at Xavier. "What was that about?"

He stared after his grandmother. "No idea."

Wide-eyed, Delia simpered over. "I'm sorry," she said. "I'm so sorry."

"Why was Grandmere so angry?"

Delia just shook her head.

"Mom!"

"I don't know." She wrung her hands. "I don't know." She shook her head. "I don't...I don't know." She kept muttering the words as she sulked from the room.

Xavier ran a hand through his thick, wavy hair. "Jesus Christ. This family..."

"I don't understand. Laurent is a Villere, and from what I—we—just...experienced, he seems pretty fond of Élise."

He muttered something, but she couldn't quite make out the words. Although she definitely heard the word, "him".

"What?"

"Nothing." He rose, his movements still a bit shaky but definitely seemed stronger than they were moments ago. He offered his hand. "C'mon."

She let him pull her to her feet, but once there, swayed unsteadily. She clutched her head. "Oh my God."

"You okay?"

"Yeah, just...weak. I'll be fine. Once I get to bed." She smiled. "My hotel sure is going to be a long walk."

"Nonsen—"

She never heard the rest of what he intended to say. She took one step and the room spun into a churning black vortex.

One minute Lottie was smiling up at him and the next she was falling face-first toward the floor. Luckily, Xavier still had her in his grasp or he might have never caught her in time.

In spite of abnormally weak and tired muscles—what the hell had that séance done to him—he was able to lift her into his arms.

"Lottie." He gave her a gentle shake. She didn't so much as twitch. Her chest rose and fell so he knew she was breathing. Passed out, but breathing.

She'd been through so much he couldn't blame her. As exhausted as his body was from just one little vision, hers must have been completely tapped out. She'd been going through this for what, two days? Three days?

A vision. Had he really experienced that? Could he deny it? Could he really look at the woman cradled in his arms and pretend he hadn't imagined the same vision she imagined?

First things first, he needed to get her to bed. There'd be time later to deny, fret, be dumbfounded by their shared experience tonight. Much later.

And he needed to get her out of this room. It churned with what felt like toxic energy, like pure, putrid hate. Whatever it was, he felt sick breathing it in.

It was a struggle, and he stumbled a few times, but he managed to carry her up to the Guest House suite. For a brief moment, he considered taking her to his bedroom, but the door wasn't lockable, at least not from the outside. And sleeping in his bedroom with him might be a little weird for her. At least in the suite, he could keep an eye on her but still be safely in another room.

He might be able to offer physical protection—well, once his strength came back, which it slowly was—but he couldn't protect her from evil he couldn't see or touch. He needed a few items from the shop for that.

The realization shocked him. That he even considered something paranormal might be threatening her went against everything he'd believed for years. Everything he'd denied. Avoided. Resisted. But what he needed to do felt natural. Right.

After tucking her into bed and checking every corner of the suite for hiding intruders, he locked the door behind him and headed for the shop. If he could have somehow connected the security chain and still made it out of the room he would have. Between Julien and Grandmere's weird behavior, he didn't trust anyone.

Speak of the devil...

Julien stood in the courtyard, smoking a cigarette.

"Did you get Miss Headcase put down for the night?" he asked, exhaling smoke into Xavier's face.

He snatched the cigarette from his brother's hand and tossed in onto the brick, extinguishing it with the sole of his boot. "What the fuck has gotten into you?"

"I'm just trying to keep you from making a huge mistake. Sam told me all about that girl. She's troubled with a capital T."

"Aren't we all."

"Not like this chick. What nonsense has she put in your head? That our great grandfather was somehow in love with her great grandmother?"

Xavier felt his eyes narrow. "How did you—"

"That little séance of yours wasn't exactly quiet."

151

Unfortunately, he couldn't respond to that. Shortly after Lottie blacked out he had followed suit. "Well, I don't see what difference it makes."

"C'mon, man. Look past your dick. She's trying to scam you."

There had been many times in Xavier's life when he'd wanted to punch his brother but always resisted. He barely kept his fist from splitting Julien's smartass lip this time. "I don't think so," he said through gritted teeth. "And if she is, it's none of your fucking business."

"Your business is my business, bro."

"Since when?" Exasperated, Xavier shook his head. Maybe Julien was high or drunk, but he was definitely acting out of character. Even his normal, slime-ball act wasn't this slimy. "By the way, give me whatever key you used to sneak into her room."

"I wasn't sneaking," Julien told him with a smirk, pulling the key from his pocket and dangling it in front of Xavier's nose. "I was investigating."

Yeah, right.

He snatched the key and headed straight for the store. He didn't have time for Julien's bullshit. Lottie was alone and vulnerable.

Before gathering his supplies he made sure to grab the master key from the office. At this point he didn't trust another living person—or dead for that matter—with it.

Lottie awoke feeling alone, empty, and strangely, well rested.

The bed she lay in was plush, lavish, and huge. She couldn't touch either edge at the same time and the velvety mattress topper made her feel like she was lying in a cloud. Above her, antique tins covered the high ceilings in beautiful, scrolling grids, broken only by the rich mahogany pillars of her bed frame and deep burgundy drapes.

Now she remembered. She must be at the Villere Guest House.

It came back to her in a rush. Being burned in the shower, Julien waiting outside, the séance, sharing the vivid erotic memory of Laurent and Élise's lovemaking with Xavier...

That was why she felt so alone and empty. She hadn't dreamed. The story always continued while she slept, but this time...nothing.

She sat upright in bed, the pit in her stomach growing deeper. What happened after that night? And why didn't Élise share it with her? Surely it didn't end there. Surely that wasn't the end of the story.

How did the children end up in St. Louis? And why did her family, starting with Amélie, the boys, and continuing up to the death of her parents, seem to be cursed with tragedy after tragedy?

She hadn't felt so alone since the morning after her parents' death. The pit grew to a chasm and she suddenly wanted to puke.

A soft snore turned her attention. Slumped in the wingback chair, one long leg draped over an arm, the other stretched out before him, Xavier slept in a position that looked crippling.

The chasm in her gut shrunk.

With a smile, she rose and approached him. He reminded her of a large, gangly puppy, all arms and legs. Okay, a large, gorgeous puppy, with deep brown eyes, and enough muscles to make any girl weak in the knees.

She remembered their kiss and bit her lip. If only that passion had been reserved for her and her alone. She knew he'd been reeling from Laurent and Élise's experience, just as she had. The passion she'd tasted, the passion she'd meant for him to taste, had been residual. It wasn't real. It couldn't be.

"Hey," she said, gently nudging him. "Wake up. You're making me sore just looking at you."

One eye cracked open.

"Good morning, sunshine," she cooed.

He rubbed a hand across his face, and then cracked the other eye. "Was I drooling?"

"A little, but I mopped it up."

Leaning back in the chair, he stretched high above his head. Not only did every bone in his body seem to crack with the effort, but the bottom of his shirt rose a good six inches and she couldn't help sneak a glimpse of his rather nice, rather well-defined abs. Actually, really nice and really defined.

She cleared her throat and took a purposeful step back. "Thanks for putting me to bed." She bit her lip. That sounded wrong. "I mean, thanks for bringing me up here. What happened? The last thing I remember is talking to you. Did I pass out or something?"

"Out cold."

"Weird."

He was stretching again and to avoid gawking at him and his amazing body, she looked the other way, like the bed somehow needed her attention.

It was then that she saw it. Dangling from the headboard was a pair of chicken feet. And there was another pair above the footboard, and a pair on the bathroom door...

"It is a little gruesome," Xavier said directly into her ear.

She jumped in spite of herself. He was standing *right* behind her.

"They're supposed to be for protection, though. You know, against evil spirits."

"I do know. Laurent hung a pair over Amélie's bed." She turned to him, surprised by how incredibly close he was. "You did all this?"

"Yeah, well, I tend to overdo it sometimes. I just thought it couldn't hurt, right?"

"No, it's nice. And I did sleep well. Too well, maybe."

He laughed. "How do you sleep too well?"

"No dreams," she replied sadly. "Every time I've gone to sleep I've dreamt of them. The story picks right up, really."

"But not last night?"

She shook her head. "Unfortunately, no."

"Maybe our ghosts were worn out. That *was* a rather intense memory." His eyebrows bobbed.

"How can you joke about such a thing? This is serious!" At least, she *thought* it was serious.

"It isn't often I share a sex dream with another person. How can one not joke about it?"

"I'm not even sure it was the same dream anymore," she said haughtily. When she realized her hands were on her hips in classic "bitch-wing" pose, she quickly dropped them. *That* was a level of immaturity she wasn't willing to cross.

"I'd be happy to reenact it with you."

"No!" But the thought made her cheeks—and other parts—warm considerably.

"For someone who wanted to convince me so badly last night she decided to tease me with a kiss, you sure are being resistant."

"That was last night."

"Well, at least let me describe it for. So you're convinced and all. Let's see, there was the make-out session in the dining room, then Laurent carried her up the stairs to the *boudoir*—"

"Okay! Yes, it's the same dream." She was pretty sure he chuckled, but chose to ignore it. Her chest was suddenly burning hot, and she rubbed a hand over it, stopping when she felt something hard.

It was a pendant. Actually, two pendants, hanging from a single silver chain. She looked down at a necklace she wasn't wearing last night. One medallion was blue and white and turquoise and looked an awful lot like an eye. The other was brass, and inscribed with a hieroglyph-like symbol. "What is this?"

"Oh, I put that on you. More protection. The top one is the vévé for Papa Damballah. It's one of Voodoo spirits, supposed to offer protection. And the other one is a Turkish evil eye. It's actually more for jealously, but you never know, we *could* have a jealous ghost on our hands."

She could no longer be mad. "Thank you."

"Now, you sure you don't want to reenact that dream. Just to make sure…"

Obviously he was messing with her. She gave him a hard look. He just grinned.

"I can't believe you're so nonchalant about all this."

He gestured toward the multitude of chicken feet hanging in the room. "Does this look nonchalant to you?"

"I mean about…what we experienced…together."

"Right." He seemed to chew on it for a moment, all the while taking her in. "You know I could really use some coffee. Wanna talk about it over a cup?"

"That sounds great. Just let me freshen up."

"Oh, I have your clothes." He dashed out of the room and returned carrying her tank and shorts in a crumpled heap. "I, um, didn't fold them or anything."

She laughed, taking the clothing from him. "That's perfectly fine. Thanks for washing them."

She noticed the chicken feet the moment she closed the bathroom door. "You hung feet from the shower too?" she called through the solid wood.

"Yeah. Didn't you have a problem in there?"

"I did." It was all she could do to keep from laughing out loud.

She quickly peed, brushed her teeth using the smallest amount of water possible, dressed, and met Xavier, courteously waiting in the sitting room and watching TV. He was constantly surprising her.

Clicking off the TV, he rose.

She handed him back his T-shirt and athletic shorts. He glanced at the neatly folded bundle. "You trying to show me up or something?"

"Folding clothes is a habit. Two or three foster moms ago," she said with a dismissive wave of her hand.

He set the clothes on the couch. "Let's go. My head's about to explode from lack of caffeine."

CHAPTER FOURTEEN

At a nearby coffee shop, they settled into a table tucked into a quiet corner, well away from other patrons. Xavier left briefly to order and returned with a tray filled with pastries and two oversized cups of coffee.

"I'm starving too," he explained as he unloaded the tray. After returning the tray to the bussing station, he sat down, took a big swig of coffee and then said, "So, back to that dream."

"You just jump right in, don't you?"

He shrugged. "Since you won't reenact it with me…"

She shook her head. "That. I seriously don't understand how you can be so chill."

"It wasn't like it was actually you and I in there. We relived an experience of our grandparents that happened hundreds of years ago. Which I admit is kinda creepy, but nothing to get worked up over."

"Yeah, but it wasn't like watching a movie. In these dreams I am Élise. I experience everything she does from her point of view. Everything."

"I get it. I saw things from my grandfather's eyes

as well."

"Doesn't that make it more...intense?"

"Sure. But I'm not him and you aren't Élise and it was still a memory."

"A very real memory."

"And a good one." He shrugged. "Besides, it wasn't even my style."

"You mean you don't make love like your grandfather."

The statement didn't even make him flinch. As weird a concept as it was. "Not at all."

"That's too bad."

His mouth fish-gaped for a moment before he seemed to recover from the shock of her retort. "Hey, I'm not saying both parties weren't satisfied..."

"An understatement."

"...I'm just saying I have my own style and set of skills."

"Ah," she murmured dismissively.

"You know you're just challenging me to prove it to you."

"Meh," she replied as blasé as possible while trying not to overheat at the thought. She quickly turned her attention to stuffing a large hunk of croissant into her mouth.

She could see in his eyes that he did, indeed, take it as a challenge. The thought made her swallow, and not just because of the croissant.

It was time to change the subject. "So what I don't get from all this, is why? Why has Élise been showing me this sliver of her life? I mean, don't get me wrong, it's been a beautiful story, but there has to be a reason."

"Maybe she wanted to bring us together."

Lottie could feel her face scrunch up in

confusion.

"I take it you don't like that explanation? What if one of our kids is destined to cure some horrible, deadly disease."

Great. So first, he didn't believe her about the ghosts and now he was teasing her about them.

She couldn't worry about it. She didn't have the energy to worry about it. He was here. He was still supporting her and at least now he believed her.

"It's got to be more than that. There has to be more. She didn't go to all this effort for nothing. I need to back to sleep. I need to figure out the rest of the story."

"You don't look very tired to me."

"I'm not. I'm wide-awake. Maybe if you knock me out..." She was only half joking.

"We can get wasted. A few hours of early morning partying always means an afternoon nap for me."

"That'd take too long. I still have one more of Amanda's pills."

"I really don't think you should take any more of those pills."

"Your concern is appreciated but I'm a big girl. I've barely taken any. Amanda pops these all the time, while drinking, while smoking..." she drifted off, her brain suddenly reminding her of something important, something she really needed to do.

"Oh my God, what time is it?"

He checked his phone. "Ten-thirty."

She jumped out of her chair, her coffee cup precariously teetering back and forth in its saucer. "Oh no."

"What's wrong?"

"My flight leaves in two hours. I can't go home.

Not yet."

"Then don't. Stay."

"What?"

His smile was hard to miss. He seemed almost delighted, relieved even.

"Change your flight. Stay. Stay with me...at the Guest House, of course."

"I don't know if I can."

"Why not? Wait...if you need help with the finances, I'll be more than happy—"

"No!" she blurted the word.

Shit. She didn't want to seem ungrateful, but money had never been an issue. The pay out from her parents' life insurance policy had her well taken care of for the rest of her life. Which was good, because her chosen field of social work—specifically working within the foster care system—wasn't exactly lucrative.

She took a breath and exhaled, sitting back down.

"No, thank you, I can cover it. It's just..."

"It's just, what? You stayed there last night. So you stay a few more days."

"I know, but what am I supposed to tell them?" It was weird that she couldn't imagine telling her friends about the crazy things that had been happening to her, yet she'd been compelled to tell Xavier barely twenty-four hours after meeting him.

"Make something up. Tell them you're not finished seeing the city."

"It's lame at best, but I guess it's not entirely a lie." She ran both hands through her hair and tried to convince herself.

What was she suddenly so afraid of? Wasn't this what she wanted? To stay. To solve the mystery. Why the hesitation? Everything she wanted was here, including the man before her.

Oh, maybe that's what it was.

Xavier's expression became hard. He must've noticed her hesitation had everything to do with him. "I don't know why you're balking now. You didn't see them all day yesterday or last night, and I haven't seen you check your messages or call or text them once."

Busted.

"I know. It just feels strange letting them leave without me. And I barely know you…"

"Seriously? That's your excuse? We're not shacking up, Lottie. I'm doing you a favor. And believe it or not, this now involves me and I'd like to get to the bottom of it, too."

Wow, he was angry. She could read it in his eyes, hear it in his tone. She wasn't sure what to make of it.

Suddenly, she wanted nothing more than to kiss him. Kiss his anger away. Maybe she could taste some of that passion from the night before.

But what if she did? Was that what she was scared of?

God, she was so confused. Confused about her past, confused about Xavier, anxious to get back to Élise, worried about what she was going to discover, afraid she actually might not dream again, frightened of whatever entity was trying to hurt her.

She rubbed her eyes wearily. "I'm sorry. You've done so much for me and I do appreciate it. This is just all so crazy and I'm a freaking mess. I feel like I'm being tossed between three different worlds and I can barely tell if I'm coming or going."

Her gaze dropped to the table where it stayed, focused on the half eaten croissant, noting how the flaky crust glistened with butter. It didn't even look good any more as her appetite had completely abandoned her.

"Hey." He bent down to peer at her. "Just stay, okay? We'll get this figured out. I want to help you, Lottie. I need to help you. And I want—" He paused and then visibly swallowed. "Hopefully we'll get this figured out soon and you can head home."

She was pretty sure that wasn't what he was originally going to say but let it go. "Sure," she said, nodding. "Thank you."

Her lips pursed tightly together, she kept nodding, like she was reminding herself she was indeed staying. "Yeah, this will be good. I just gotta get my luggage, and...yeah."

He rose. "Great. Let's go."

She hesitated. "Xavier, this is probably something I should handle by myself."

"I'm not going to let you jump into that tank of sharks alone," he scoffed.

His comment caught her off guard. "What do you mean, 'let me'?"

"I'm not going to abandon you."

Her eyebrows bunched together. How was he possibly abandoning her...

"I'll be fine. Really. I just need to be alone for a minute. Figure out what I'm going to tell them. I'll meet you back at the house."

"Who is going to carry your suitcase?"

"I managed to carry my suitcase to the hotel without your help. I'm pretty sure I can manage now." It came out snottier than she intended.

"No way. I let you walk out of the bar the other night with your drunk-ass friend and I about had a nervous breakdown worrying about you. Not going to happen again."

There was that word again, "let".

The air in the room was suddenly very hot, stifling-hot, like she was swimming-in-lava-hot. Her chest squeezed tight and her lungs were doing their best impression of deflated balloons.

It was too much. It was all too much. She needed time to think about...everything. Having him there would just distract her. And the last thing she needed was him bossing her around.

She rose and headed for the door. "I gotta get out of here."

"Lottie, wait..."

Ignoring him, she yanked open the door, quickly shutting it—and him—behind her.

Anxious to put as much distance between herself and the café, she flew down the sidewalk with a quicker than usual stride, even jumping into the street when she needed to get around a slow moving tourist group blocking her way.

Xavier. Damnit, why did he have to be so infuriating? Maybe he meant well and all, but Jesus, it was overwhelming. Hardly anyone had given two shits about her well-being for years. For him to run in on his white horse...it was damn near suffocating.

Especially now. Especially with all the other shit going on. Especially when he decided to give her *permission.*

She sure as hell didn't need it and hadn't asked for it. In fact, she hadn't asked for any of this. Didn't want it. Maybe she should just go to the airport with her friends and take the flight home.

The hotel was inches away by the time she realized she was even close. Pausing, she slammed her hand into her purse, quickly locating the key-card to her room before continuing at her brisk pace.

It seemed like ages since she'd arrived four days ago. She'd felt like an entirely different person then, with few worries other than trying to have a good time, and making sure Sam and Amanda didn't have too much fun and wind up in a ditch.

And now, she was unbelievably being haunted by the great grandmother she never knew she had and something far more sinister. She couldn't deny she wanted answers, craved them actually. But at what cost? How bad would it be if she just walked away and left all of this all behind? All of it. New Orleans, Élise, the apparent curse, the Villeres—each and every one of them.

The thought punched a hole in her gut. She shoved it aside as she pushed the key-card in the slot. The green light came on at the same moment she turned the lever and started to open the door, only to promptly shut it.

There was no way she was prepared to face them. First, she needed to pull her shit together. If she went in there in her current state, they'd rip her to shreds. What had Xavier called them, "sharks"? It was appropriate.

Taking a few moments to roll the tension out of her shoulders, she mentally prepared her lie. She'd use the excuse suggested by Xavier. It was plausible. Unlikely but plausible.

Lining the card with the lock and pushing it forward, she put on her game face and whispered, "Here goes nothing."

"Hey!" she said nonchalantly when she stepped into the common room of their suite. Music blared and both girls had Daiquiris in hand. Their heads jerked up.

Amanda jumped to her feet. Sam promptly

returned her attention to her phone.

"Where the hell have you been?" Even with the auto-tuned voice of the top-forty singer belting it out in the background, Amanda's voice sounded shrill. "I've been texting the shit out of you. Our flight leaves in like, barely an hour. We were about ready to leave without you."

Lottie offered a laissez-faire smile. "Yeah…you guys go ahead. I canceled my flight. I'm staying here for a more few days."

"You what!"

That was so high-pitched, Lottie cringed.

"Why?"

A sarcastic grunt came from Sam, who never took her eyes off her phone.

She ignored it. "You know," she said lightly. "I'm really enjoying New Orleans and would like to see more of the city."

Another snort came from Sam. "I think Lottie has a boyfriend," she said.

Lottie resisted the urge to hurl her purse at her.

Amanda looked at Sam and back to Lottie again. "Wait a minute! Are you staying because of that Voodoo guy? What was his name…?"

"Xavier Villere," Sam quickly shot off.

"No. I'm not staying because of him. I told you, I just want to check out more of the city. The history of this place fascinates me," which, of course, wasn't a lie, "and I was told I should visit Oak Alley, an old antebellum sugar plantation."

"And you expect us to buy that shit? I know you stayed with Xavier last night."

Once again, she ignored Sam, keeping her gaze firmly on Amanda.

"Did you really?" Amanda wondered.

"Yeah, but it isn't what you think."

"That sucks because he's hot."

In spite of her topsy-turvy, chaotic emotional state, she couldn't help smiling at that obvious statement. "Anyway, I'll be home in a few days."

"What are you going to do about classes? They start in two freaking days."

"I don't know. I'm honestly not really worried about school at the moment."

"Clearly."

"Yeah, lucky for you, your parents left you a small fortune. You can afford it, right Lottie?" Sam's smile was saccharin-sweet and just as fake.

"What does that have to do with anything?"

Finally, she set her phone down and approached them. "I am so sick of your shit. Your, 'oh I'm *so* tragic because my parents died' bullshit routine when they left you a mint. And how you're always ragging on us for drinking too much or hooking up with guys when I've seen you puke more than a few times in my day, and I *know* you've had a couple of one-night stands. And here you are immediately shacking up with the first hot guy that pays you any attention. Just because you like to think you've had such a hard life and that you've somehow got it more figured out than the rest of us doesn't mean you have. You're such a fucking hypocrite."

"I—"

"Just admit it, Lottie! Admit you're staying here because of some cock. I might actually respect you then."

"Screw you," was the most clever comeback Lottie could come up with.

Ducking into the bedroom, she yanked her suitcase from the dresser and packed her few belongings as quickly as possible before heading back into the sitting room and straight for the door. Her fingers were on the handle when Amanda stopped her.

"Lottie, wait. Where are you going? Really."

"None of your—" She took a deep breath and reigned in her anger as much as she could. "I'm checking into another room. I'll text you later."

With a hug, Amanda whispered, "Make sure you do. See you in a few."

CHAPTER FIFTEEN

She felt like she was dragging a dead body instead of a twenty-pound roller as she lugged her suitcase through the courtyard, down the long, narrow hall, through the foyer, and out into the bright sun. Blinded by its brightness, she squinted as she dug in her purse for her sunglasses. Why on earth did she bury them in her purse?

What a mess. What a fucking, awful mess. She just wanted to curl up in a ball and cry. She didn't even know why she was so bothered by Sam's comments. They'd never been that close, but she hadn't realized Sam hated her so much. No, more like despised, loathed, detested. She'd actually thought of Sam as her friend.

Maybe what was worse is she knew Sam's accusations weren't off base. She was far from perfect, yet she constantly chastised those around her. Even Xavier. Especially Xavier.

She felt a tear slide down her cheek. God, none of this crying bullshit. She didn't need that, not now.

"Where are those fucking sunglasses?!"

When digging through her purse returned

nothing, she squatted down and dumped the contents on the dirty sidewalk. Her wallet, a compact, some crumpled up receipts, a comb, lip-gloss, but no. Fucking. Sunglasses.

She was ready to chuck the empty purse across the street and then throw herself on the ground and have a good old-fashioned tantrum, when a large, strong hand rested gently on her shoulder.

Xavier knelt beside her, lifting the sunglasses from where they'd been the whole time—perched on her head—and handing them to her. He didn't say a word as he began retrieving the discarded items of her purse.

"What are you doing here? I thought I told you—"

"I know," he interjected quietly. "But this is the man I am, Lottie. I can't sit by and watch those I care about suffer. Not when I might be able to help. I realize it can be stifling, but I can't be any other way."

She could no longer breathe. And not because he was stifling.

He continued to reload her purse. Speechless, all she could do was watch. Like her lungs and her voice box no longer functioned.

Did he say he cared about her? Was that what she heard?

As much as she felt like she couldn't read him, or that he looked at her like he couldn't figure out what to do with her, he'd still been nothing but helpful, thoughtful, and attentive.

And yes, maybe she'd been momentarily overwhelmed by his desire to…protect. But that's because there was something wrong with her, not him.

Even the way he retrieved the contents of her purse, the care he took placing each item back in her bag... It made her throat tighten and chest constrict.

Feeling dumbfounded, she mechanically took back her purse when he handed it to her.

"So I was thinking," he said, taking her hand and pulling her to her feet, "that while we're waiting for you to be tired enough to nap, we could hit a second-line parade. There's one rolling out of Treme here shortly."

Standing before him, her body inches from his, her hand wrapped in his strong but gentle grip, her mind still stuttering, she reached up with her free hand and clasped the back of his neck. Extending onto her tiptoes, she pulled him to her and covered his full lips in the softest, sweetest kiss she could manage. No tongue, nothing debaucherous, only her lips pressed against his.

He immediately pulled her closer, his arm wrapping around the small of her back. His moan of approval was so delicate, so subdued, she couldn't hear it, only feel it as it vibrated her lips.

Shyness took over as she pulled away and out of his grasp.

He was grinning. "I take it you like the second-line suggestion."

"Sounds fun." Honestly, she'd never heard of a second-line parade, but since Xavier suggested it, she was all in.

"Perfect. Let's just drop off your suitcase." Grabbing the roller, he turned toward the direction of the Guest House.

"Xavier," she called and he turned back to her. "I'm sorry for—"

"Nothing. There's nothing to be sorry for."

"Thank you."

He glanced at the suitcase. "Of course."

"No. Well, for that too, but for everything else. For being here."

He shrugged. "I wouldn't be anywhere else."

She could hear the music a block before they reached the parade, which was nothing like she was expecting. No long line of floats progressing slowly down spectator lined streets. There *was* a small float, and a few people lingered on front porches, but the parade was actually a mass of several hundred people marching down the street. A brass band marched with them—or so she heard. She could only see the tip of a sousaphone. The actual band was obscured by the crowd around them.

They joined at the back of the moving mob, a few feet in front of the police horses.

"Want a beer?" Xavier asked.

"I don't know…" She fiddled with the hem of her skirt. She was glad they'd had time for her to change before catching up with the parade. She didn't think she could stand to be in those clothes for five more minutes.

"Nothing says 'afternoon nap' like day drinking."

"That's true. Though I *do* still have some of Amanda's pills..."

His look was disapproving. She had to admit, she really didn't want to trudge through the post-Amanda-pill-fog again.

"Okay, okay. No pills. A beer sounds great."

Xavier headed into the crowd where he stopped a man wheeling a large ice chest. Still walking, the man dipped into the cooler and produced two cans of beer. Xavier paid him and returned to her side. After

172

handing her one of the ice-cold cans, he popped the top on his and took a huge swig.

She glanced at the officers behind her. She knew drinking on the street was perfectly legal in New Orleans, but she was pretty sure selling beer out of a cooler wasn't. They didn't seem to notice or care. The smell of Marijuana hung in the air and that didn't faze them either.

"Nothing beats a second-line beer," Xavier said. "C'mon, let's get closer to the band." Taking her hand, he wove through the crowd, pulling her behind him until they were right next to the boisterous group of trumpet, trombone, saxophone, sousaphone players, and drummers. Directly in front of them were a group of men, young and old, dressed in bright green suits. Some carried staffs with huge green feather toppers, dripping with beads and glitter, but all danced, their feet a flurry of fast steps, dips, and spins.

The crowd around them danced as well. Some just marched with upbeat steps and bodies that pumped back and forth, some busted out fancy footwork rivaling the costumed dancers.

Including Xavier. He stepped, kicked, spun, and twisted with the best of them. His athletic body strong and powerful, yet smooth and graceful at the same time. It only took Lottie a half a beer to join in. Being so close to the band and being surrounded by so many dancers and so much energy, it was virtually impossible not to.

They followed the parade for several hours, weaving through local neighborhood streets and sometimes occupying entire lanes of wide, tree-lined boulevards. There were stops along the way where people sold food out of trucks or huge smoker grills, and guys with loudspeakers announced the contents of full bars set up on the roof of their pickup trucks. By the time they peeled away from the parade, now twice as big as it had been when they started, Lottie had learned a few snazzy dance moves from Xavier, was enjoying a light buzz, a belly full of a pork chop sandwich and sausage smothered in barbeque sauce, and a bladder about to burst.

She hadn't thought of Élise or Laurent or Amanda or Sam once.

"So, you think you're ready for that afternoon nap now?" he asked as they climbed the stairs to the Guest House suite.

On cue she yawned and they both laughed. "After I use the restroom, yes."

He unlocked the door and held it open. She rushed past only to pause at the bedroom door. Another pair of fowl feet hung from the door like a grotesque wreath, only this pair was four times as big as the other. She glanced at Xavier in question. "Dare I ask?"

"Turkey feet. They're bigger, so I thought they might protect the whole room."

She turned back to the talons. Black and twisted with long, sharp nails, they were straight out of a horror movie. She couldn't believe something so awful was meant to protect. The only thing beautiful about them was the symbol scrolling across the top of each gnarled foot. It was the same as the symbol etched onto her necklace—the véve of Papa Damballah.

Even though her bladder was pleading with her to hurry up, she continued to linger. "The feet... So, I know they're a protective charm to ward off evil spirits. But what about good spirits?"

"I don't know. To be honest, twenty-four hours ago I just thought they were disgusting good-luck

174

charms for superstitious old women, and trinkets to
sell to tourists. After last night...well, I decided there
might be more merit to the superstition. If anything, it
couldn't hurt."

"What if there's too much protection?"

"You think the feet might be why you didn't
dream about Élise?"

"Maybe..."

"Well, you're welcome to crash in my room. No
chicken feet in there."

"That might not be a bad idea. Just in case, of
course." Reaching up, her fingers touched the Papa
Damballah necklace.

"It might be all you'll need for protection," he
nodded toward the necklace. "Besides, I'll be close."

His grin was nothing short of mischievous,
drawing her gaze to his lips. She could get caught up
in those.

He turned toward the door. "Follow me,
Madame."

"Oh, hang on. Let me use the restroom first."

"We have a couple in the house."

"I like this one. The severed feet really add a
touch of class."

"I'll remember that."

His bedroom was one of several on the second
floor and faced the street. A door leading out to the
wrought iron balcony was open, allowing a warm
breeze to buzz through the room.

"Glad I picked up before you saw what a slob I
can be," he said, snatching a few discarded pieces of
clothing from the floor and tossing them into a
hamper.

She took in the entire room before she'd stepped
two feet into it. Black and white framed

photographs—new mixed with old scenes of New Orleans, including a very old looking picture of the Villere House—hung on the cool, gray painted walls. Antique cameras and hardback books topped the shelves of a bookcase adjacent to a computer work-station, and records filled the lower shelves. The bed was neatly made and looked way too inviting. She yawned again.

Besides the few pieces of clothing, the room was spotless. He was no "slob".

He held out his hands like a game-show hostess. "Welcome to my humble abode."

"'Tis very nice." She bowed her head and flipped her hand extravagantly. "Did you do the decorating?"

"Collaborative effort with a college friend. Same with the Guest House. Sophie has an amazing eye for these things. I'm just lucky she cuts me a deal."

It was the first time he'd ever mentioned a female other than his mother or grandmother. She was shocked by the way she bristled at the innocent mention.

She turned her attention to the wall covered in photos.

"These are cool. You take them?"

"I wasn't alive in the 19th Century, Lottie," he said with perfect seriousness.

"The ones from *this* century." She kind of wanted to add, "asshat" to the end of that statement, but wasn't sure if they were on that level of kidding around or not.

"No, my father did...years ago. After he left, I rescued them from my mother who tried to throw everything out, including the cameras."

"So they're a remembrance to him?"

"You could say that. I don't particularly miss him.

176

He skipped out the minute things got tough and didn't bother checking up on us until things got better. But I think it's important to hang onto parts of him. The good parts."

She walked around the room, running her fingers along the bookshelves and reading the hardback labels. She spotted an old turntable on the middle shelf she hadn't noticed on her initial room scan. Made sense with all the records...

When she looked up, Xavier was just steps behind her. Was she making him uncomfortable by looking at all his stuff?

"I assume this actually plays albums," she said lightly.

"If not, I've been doing it wrong." He winked. "Need a little mood music for your nap?"

"That would be great."

"Any requests?"

"DJ's choice."

He thumbed through the records, selected one, pulled it out, looked it over, and then placed it on the platter.

"Louie Armstrong. Nice."

"One thing we're good at in New Orleans is appreciating our history."

"Except you," she said earnestly.

His brows pushed together until there was barely a millimeter between them.

"You seem to spend a lot of time denying your heritage," she added.

"What? You saw the chicken feet, right?"

Oh good. He wasn't annoyed by her comment. She sometimes had that effect on people. Thinking about Sam, she realized she often had that effect.

"How could I miss them?" Sitting on the bed, she

began removing her shoes. She should probably feel weird sleeping in his bed but didn't. Maybe the years of drifting from foster home to foster home had numbed her, but the idea of sleeping in his bed felt completely natural.

She lay back on the pillows. He still stood off to the side, watching her. When she glanced his direction he quickly looked away.

"Well, I need to get some work done. Will the computer bother you?"

She had to admit she was a bit disappointed he wasn't joining her. But then what? Were they supposed to spoon or something?

"Not at all."

He kept his gaze firmly averted as he sat at the desk. "Cool. Well, sweet dreams."

Was he feeling awkward because she was there, or because he wanted her there but didn't want to make her uncomfortable? Should she just ask him to join her? Should she just walk over to his desk and wrap her arms around those broad shoulders? Maybe she could kiss the back of his neck, slide her hands down the front of his shirt. She could imagine the feel of his firm skin under her palms, the heat of his skin, his large body above her, inside her…

An orgasm would make napping even easier.

She bit her lip. Should she?

Closing her eyes, she envisioned the scenario, the temperature in her body rising to a near boil. She mentally played it out, savoring every detail. His lips on her skin, her legs wrapped around his trim waist as he slid in and out of her over and over and over…God, the images felt so real, she could actually taste him. Just like her dreams.

Wait, was she sleeping? It was an odd question to

pose and should indicate she was actually awake, but the moment she asked it she realized she was in that weird state between being awake and fully asleep, and as much as she wanted to make her fantasies a reality and mount the gorgeous man sitting feet from her, she knew she needed to succumb to slumber. Élise needed her, Laurent needed her, and she needed them. She was certain Xavier would still be there when she woke.

Xavier hadn't registered a single word he'd read on his laptop monitor. And he'd read it twice. Reading comprehension was out of the question with Lottie sleeping in his bed and inches from his chair.

Goddamn, he wanted to join her. Wanted to curl his body around hers and let her blond curls caress his face. And he wasn't even tired.

But he had no business climbing in that bed with her. She was confused enough as it was. Besides the overwhelming mind-fuck that must come from living the reality of long dead ancestors at night and then being haunted by them during the day, discovering the existence of said ancestors, and then her awful friends, he was pretty certain she was confusing the lingering feelings Élise Cantrelle's ghost had for his grandfather with feelings for him.

Even though she'd kissed him three times now, twice were under the influence of Élise. This afternoon showed promise but he wanted her head to be clear before he started seducing her. He needed to know that she wanted him not Laurent Villere reincarnated.

He had to admit even he was confused. Not about

his feelings for the woman in his bed. The way he felt about her had nothing to do with his grandfather. Perhaps it had contributed to his initial interest, but it quickly ended there. He wasn't as consumed by the past as Lottie was. And he was able to separate himself from it. He wasn't sure she could do the same. Yet.

But even if his desire for her wasn't adding to his own mind-fuckedness, everything he'd ever believed, or not believed, had changed in twenty-four hours. He still hadn't fully processed the previous evening's events. How the hell could he? He wouldn't deny it had happened or deny all that weirdness at the séance with the room shaking and lights flickering had happened. But Jesus…ghosts?

And his mom actually conjured them. All these years, he just thought she was nuts. Man, he wasn't winning any son-of-the-year awards any time soon.

With a sigh, he pushed away from the computer and let his head fall back on the chair. If he strained his eyes, he could just make out the soft curve of Lottie's body. He hoped she was dreaming and he hoped as hell it was good and she was getting the answers she needed.

His fears were it wasn't. Something very angry didn't like her and might even be trying to hurt her.

He hoped this shit would be over soon. He wanted her safe, he wanted her happy, but he also wanted her. He might want to give her space while she sorted everything out, but it definitely was *not* easy. And if she kissed him again like she'd kissed him this morning, there wouldn't be a millimeter of space between them.

CHAPTER SIXTEEN

She was surrounded by darkness so thick it seeped through her skin into her very bones, clogging her arteries and filling her lungs.

Breathe. She couldn't breathe!

Frantically, she began flailing her arms, desperate to push through the deepening darkness. It only swooshed around her, sliding its inky tendrils through her hair and softly caressing her skin.

More of it filled her lungs, choking her, killing her.

Far above her head a light slowly appeared, burning through the black. Just beyond the shimmering layers of black was Xavier, his hand held out for her. With every ounce of her waning energy, she tried to swim to him. But with every kick of her feet or push with her arms, she was dragged down deeper.

Xavier reached into the abyss, reached for her. His face slowly changed and it wasn't Xavier, but Laurent. "Take my hand," he said.

She wanted to, oh how she wanted to, but she couldn't. She tried to scream that desire, but nothing

181

but gurgles escaped, and more of the darkness filled her lungs.

Laurent, no Xavier now, reached further into the liquid. He almost had her, the tips of his fingers brushed hers. He was Laurent again, his face full of sadness. And then he was back to being Xavier. Dipping his torso into the darkness he lunged for her.

But just as his hand grabbed hers, everything changed.

The inky blackness slipped away and Xavier's face melted into something horrible, grotesque. Only his eyes remained the same. At least they were similar to his eyes. So dark they were nearly black but filled with nothing but hatred. She'd seen them before but couldn't remember where.

Talons replaced his hands as whatever replaced Xavier pinned her to the ground. The melted face leaned close and slowly began to peel away, dripping onto her until nothing but a skull remained. She tried to pull away, jerking and twisting with all her might. But the more she jerked against the monster's grasp, the more its talons dug into her skin until blood flowed freely from her body.

The bony jaw hinged wide and a snake slid from the opening. "You cannot have him," it hissed. "You cannot have her."

"I don't—"

"GET OUT!" A flash of a woman's face burned her retinas and then the monster flung her aside.

Lottie woke with a start, jerking up into a sitting position. She was sweating. Not a pleasant, dewy, flushed sweat either. But a dripping, pretty-sure-the-sheets-were-soaked, kind of sweat.

She must have made some noise when waking because even though Xavier had his back to her, he immediately left the computer desk and sat on the bed beside her.

"What is it? Did you—"

She shook her head furiously and tried to clear the images from her mind.

"But you dreamed, right?"

"A nightmare. A horrible nightmare." Staring at a spot on the carpet, she ran her hands through her hair, clutching the strands at the back of her neck. "Something's wrong."

He slid his arm around her shoulders and pulled her close. The gesture felt good, natural, and she rested her head on his shoulder. "What do you mean?" he asked.

"It just feels wrong. Everything feels wrong. Even now there's this ickyness to the air."

His arm tensed like he was going to remove it. "Oh, not you!" she said. The muscles relaxed and she nestled deeper into him. "I feel like she's trying to tell me something, something awful."

"Élise?"

"Yeah. But she was interrupted... God, Xavier. I don't know what to do. I *know* they're reaching out to us for a reason. But why?"

"I think you're right. My grandmother knows something—and maybe even my mother—but they aren't sharing. In fact, I'd say they're hiding something."

She lifted her head from his shoulder to look at him. "I have to find out what's going on. I won't be able to let it go."

"I understand. I feel the same way."

183

"What do we do?"

"As much as I'd love to say we can find answers here, I don't think that's going to happen."

"So, you feel it too?"

"What you're feeling? Probably not exactly, but I can tell you right now I don't trust my grandmother or my brother, and I've never felt that way before."

An idea hit her and she lifted from his embrace. "What about the vampire bar?"

"*La Luxure*?"

"That was Élise's house and the owner knew about her."

"Doesn't surprise me, actually."

Was that because the owner—Armand, right?— was a real vampire and actually knew Élise in the day? She didn't want to think about it.

"You think he'd help us?"

"He'd probably get a kick out of it."

Because he'd find it amusing *educating* the human peons? Oh, what did she care.

"Can we go there?"

He glanced at his watch. "Yes."

Opening the door revealed his mother, wide-eyed and framed by wild hair. Those black eyes darted back and forth frantically before she squeezed past them into his bedroom.

"Can I come in?" she asked after she was already in the middle of the room.

"Sure?" Xavier closed the door.

"Close the door," she said.

Lottie was pretty sure she heard him sigh.

"What's up, mom?"

Delia looked over one shoulder and then over the other. She did it two more times before sprinkling salt in a circle around her and then dribbling some in her hair. Only then did she even look at Lottie. "I have something for you." She held out a silver chain with a light green crystal dangling from the end. "Come inside the circle to take it from me, but don't break the line."

After glancing quickly at Xavier, who wore an exasperated expression on his face, Lottie carefully stepped over the white line to stand uncomfortably close to Delia. She had definitely invaded the other woman's *bubble*. Well, hers for that matter too.

Delia placed the necklace in Lottie's hand. "*You* need to put it on for it to work," she said, her face incredibly close.

"What is it?"

"Apophyllite. It's one of the best crystals for communicating with spirits. It connects you with them and also helps you remember dreams that contain messages from the other side. It has a lot of other properties but those are the ones I'm sure you're most interested in."

"Thank you." Lottie slipped the necklace around her neck, fiddled briefly with the clasp before securing it.

"Good thing you have those too." She tapped the Papa Damballah disk and the evil eye. "Maybe it'll help keep the *bad* spirits at bay."

Lottie nodded. Staying away from whatever evil trying to hurt her was high on her priority list. Even though the pendants hadn't seemed to help during her nightmares, she wasn't taking them off.

"What do you know, mom?" Xavier asked, his voice stern.

Delia just shook her head furiously.

"Mom. This is important."

His tone made her cringe and she just continued

to shake her head.

She seemed so upset, so scared, and she obviously felt like she was risking something coming here, Lottie decided to do something out of character. She embraced the other woman. "Thank you so much. I really do appreciate it."

"I wish I could do more for you. I really, really do," Delia said, hugging her back with worried urgency that bordered on desperation. It felt so motherly, so nice. Even if she wasn't Lottie's mother, it had been so long since she'd experienced that sensation of a mother's worry and concern, it brought tears to her eyes.

Pulling back shyly, Lottie wiped her eyes. She clutched the crystal pendant. "No, this is wonderful. And the séance…"

Delia shook her head again and averted her eyes. Lottie couldn't imagine what had her so scared. Well, she could, but she'd rather not.

Careful not to disturb the salt, she stepped out of the circle and turned to Xavier, who was looking at her funny. In fact, he seemed to be frowning. Was he angry with her? Maybe she'd upset Delia…

Without stepping over the salt, he reached forward and gave his mother a quick, tense hug. "Thanks, mom. I appreciate it as well."

Her expression flashed surprise and then softened to glowing happiness. "You guys should go. She doesn't like Lottie here."

"She? Grandmere?"

The head shaking resumed.

"All right," Xavier said defeated. He planted a peck on Delia's cheek and then turned to Lottie. "I guess that means we should get out of here."

"Be careful," Delia called as they left the room.

186

There was an undeniable energy in the hallway. Like the precursor to a thunderstorm, it hung heavily in the air. Warning, threatening.

Lottie glanced at Xavier, whose eyebrows were firmly knitted.

"You feel it too?"

His answer was to take her hand. She loved touching him, loved the way his hand dwarfed hers in size.

Whatever was causing the bad energy did not love it.

The feeling of foreboding increased until her stomach hurt with anxiety and every hair on her arms and neck stood at attention. Xavier gripped her hand tighter. They began to descend the old wooden staircase, the hall light surging as they passed.

It was worse on the first floor, like walking into a room filled with corpses. She was beginning to feel nauseated. Like the worst kind of stage fright, or when you knew you needed to have a serious conversation with someone where one or both of you would cry. Sick-to-your-stomach-ready-to-puke nauseated.

Xavier took one look at her face and immediately put his arm around her. The lights surged and the feeling got worse. She covered her mouth.

"I've got to get out of here," she said.

"I feel you."

They were in the same room as the séance and quickly passed through heavy French doors, emerging in a room filled with Voodoo paraphernalia. At one end sat an altar; she could see the telltale candles and various trinkets scattered on a rich, velvet table cloth. A portrait sat in the middle—a shrine to whatever spirit the altar worshipped.

She was afraid to see whose image was in that

frame. Afraid to see Sanite Villere's evil black eyes looking back at her.

Even though the lights flickered all around them and the air was as putrid as a sewage plant, Xavier paused at the altar. He pulled some coins from his pocket and tossed them into the basket.

"Do you have something to offer? In case it helps…"

She looked at him in question and then forced herself to look at the portrait. "Laurent!" she gasped.

Staring back at from a faded painting was the man who had haunted her dreams and made her great-grandmother fall in love again.

"Of course. I think it's probably a good idea to get him on our side. Giving a spirit gifts is supposed to strengthen them."

If she could have dumped her entire inheritance into that basket she would have. Instead she quickly removed her earrings and tossed them inside.

The room began to shake. Wall decorations clattered on the wall, some falling off their hangers onto the floor. In the kitchen she heard the shattering of dishes.

Wrapping his arm even tighter around her, he ushered her from the room, through a rattling beaded curtain and into the store.

"What the hell?"

She followed his line of sight and saw Sanite's altar ablaze in a glory of dozens of flickering candles.

"Hang on, I have an idea." Releasing her, he dashed over to the altar and started blowing out candles. The trembling in the room increased. Merchandise fell off shelves, books toppled to the floor, more dishes shattered in the other room… She imagined it was like being in an earthquake.

Lottie joined him and together they extinguished all the candles. Xavier then tossed the basket and the portrait aside. All at once a gust of air exploded through the room. She ducked as items flew past her head.

And then it was over.

They knelt there a moment, Xavier's body covering and shielding hers. Her head pressed to his chest, she breathed in his scent, letting the strength of his body and his desire to protect her soothe her galloping heart.

Finally he sat upright and she followed him. He took in the scene, as did she. It looked like a tornado had passed through.

"All right, that might have been a bad idea." Standing, he offered his hand.

"You're telling me." She placed her hand in his and he pulled her to her feet.

"So, you ready to hit the vampire bar now?" he asked with a grin.

She had no idea how to answer that, so she just followed his lead. "Why not?" she said nonchalantly. "What's the worst that can happen?"

CHAPTER SEVENTEEN

The walk to *La Luxure* was hurried and without words. Lottie felt that same urgent tug that had first pulled her into Villere House of Voodoo and had no doubts they were headed in the right direction. Xavier kept her hand firmly in his the entire time, easing any and all trepidation she had about returning to the vampire bar. Even as they walked down the narrow brick alley to the obscure entrance, even as he reached for the door handle…

Besides, it was too early for vampires. Right…?

It wasn't until he let go of her hand and opened the door that her heart remembered vampires were dangerous. Suddenly needing reassurance, she looked up into his dark brown eyes.

"Don't be nervous. I'm packing stakes. Long, wooden stakes."

The joke helped soothe her tension. She grinned. "So you aren't just happy to see me…."

He burst out laughing. That he seemed so relaxed made her relax, and laughing about it made her feel much better as he guided her through the open door. The club being virtually empty helped, too.

A slender woman with dark hair tended bar and a few patrons lingered on barstools. Armand sat against the far wall, blending almost perfectly with the black background. When he saw them, he rose and approached, stopping a good three feet away.

"Xavier Villere," he said fondly. It was a greeting that should have come with a handshake but didn't. "What brings you here?"

Xavier's hand slid to the small of her back. Protective, even though the gesture presented her as the reason they'd come. In spite of her earlier freak out over his desire to *protect*, she found she liked the feel of him protecting her, especially in this context. Now that she understood his nature a little better it was easier to accept his nurturing.

"Ah," Armand said. "Lottie...Boyd, correct?"

"You have a good memory." Her smile trembled but she tried to breathe through it.

"You did run out of here like the place was on fire."

Her cheeks warmed. A joking, teasing vampire. How odd.

"What can I do for you two? Would you care for a drink?"

"No, thank you," Xavier said. "We're actually here because of Élise Cantrelle." He glanced at her, a silent encouragement for her to pick up the story.

"We found out she is my great-great, well, grandmother. And, I don't know how to say this without sounding crazy, but I think she's been haunting me. Like trying to tell me something through dreams. That's what led me here the other night. The house was familiar."

"Makes sense."

That was easy. Though, what did she expect?

191

"So, what brings you back here tonight?"

"The dreams have stopped. I was hoping...well, I hoped maybe I could look around, see if something triggers my memory."

"Of course."

She glanced around the bar. There wasn't much to see there. She could see evidence of the old house, just as she had the other night, but nothing new.

"Anything?" Xavier asked.

Shaking her head, she turned back to Armand, who was watching her. God he had intense eyes. She swallowed, unable to stealth the sound.

"Um, do you think...Would it be possible..."

"Care if we go upstairs?" Xavier interjected. He sure knew how to read her, and when she was nervous or felt unsure, he jumped right in.

"Not at all."

"If it isn't too much trouble," she interjected quickly. Last thing she wanted to do was insult a vampire.

Armand's small smile revealed the points of his very sharp looking canines. "None."

He turned and started for the back room when a deafening slam came from the entrance. Julien Villere sauntered into the bar. His eyes were conniving, the irises filled in with blackness. Didn't he have green eyes? From where she stood, they looked as dark as Xavier's.

"What the fuck." Xavier's expression was a mix of shock, fury, suspicion, and bewilderment. "Did you follow us?"

"Surprise!" Julien held out his arms like he was the birthday cake. "I thought I'd see what all the fuss was with this *vampire* bar. Do I have to give it to get it, or can I just order a shot of A-positive straight up?"

Out of nowhere, the huge, muscled bartender from the other night shoved his way through the velvet curtains leading to the backroom. Lottie remembered the stacks of beer boxes lining the storeroom walls and imagined the rhino of a man now blocking Julien's path into the bar slinging them around like they were boxes of Kleenex.

She watched Xavier flinch with disgust and then take a deep breath and shake it off.

Armand's quiet presence was a startling addition. "Isn't that your brother?" he asked, his deep voice cool, but definitely irritated.

"Yes," Xavier admitted through gritted teeth.

"I will forgive him because he is a Villere, but I will not tolerate such disrespect—even from a Villere. Take care of it or I will. Or Slade will. Neither outcome will be good."

Slade must be the scowling man with his tree-trunk arms crossed tightly across his massive chest.

"Gladly." Xavier turned to her. "Why don't you go ahead while I address this...situation."

"Are you sure?" The idea of traveling upstairs alone with Armand was nothing short of terrifying.

He grabbed her hand and gave it a brief squeeze. "Absolutely."

Her lip was so firmly between her teeth as he turned away it was quite possible blood was dripping down her chin and she'd never know it. She was pretty sure Armand would...

"Don't worry," the vampire said right into her ear. "I rarely bite."

She nearly jumped out of her skin. She stared at Xavier in horror but he was already walking away. Turning to Armand, she forced a smile. He wore a mischievous half-cocked grin on his full lips.

Jesus, if there was ever a poster-boy for a vampire, he was it.

Xavier's attention was firmly on Julien and she knew enough about the man to know if he wasn't concerned about Armand neither should she.

Still...

Her eyes drifted over his solid, muscular form, sleeve tattoo, black painted nails, pale skin and bright hazel eyes. He was scary enough whether or not he was a vampire.

"Lead the way," she said with a nervous chuckle.

She followed him through the velvet curtains into the backroom, past his office, and then up stairs that were all too familiar. With a light touch, she lovingly ran her hand up the mahogany railing. She remembered this wood well. It had barely changed.

"I'm afraid I told you all I know the other night," Armand said as he opened the door at the top of the stairs. "My family merely purchased the home."

"So you didn't know Élise?"

Holding the door open for her, Armand cocked his head ever so slightly, a small smile on his lips. "No."

That was disappointing.

His apartment was not. Quite frankly, it was a little more modern than what she expected from a vampire, but definitely sleek and sexy. The main room had been completely opened up and housed a very *clean*, very high-end kitchen (strange for a vampire), with a large granite island lined with barstools—all adjacent to a living room filled with sleek leather furniture and large T.V.

"Oh."

"You sound dismayed."

"It looks nothing like I remember."

"No, it wouldn't I'm afraid. I did a complete renovation recently. The third floor remains mostly untouched. Would you like to see it?"

She shook her head. "I don't know. I never made it up there in any of my dreams. I was hoping something would trigger a memory." Looking around the room, she tried to envision the second floor when it had been Élise's house, but couldn't. It was just too different.

"What is that crystal you keep stroking?"

Oh? Was she? She hadn't noticed. Looking down she saw the green pendant between her fingers. Embarrassed, she dropped her hand. "Nervous habit, I guess."

"Is that Apophyllite?"

"Yeah. Delia Villere gave it to me to, you know, help channel Élise's spirit. But obviously it isn't working."

"These things can be tricky. Do you have anything personal of hers—Élise's?"

Lottie felt her heart jump with excitement. Was he about to tell her he hand an old scarf or something he'd found in the attic…? "No. Do you?"

"That would be convenient, but no." He paused, seemed to think for a moment, and then gestured toward one of the barstools. "Would you like to sit?"

"I'm fine. I should probably just go back downstairs."

"Perhaps you should sit." It was definitely a command and she wasn't prepared to argue. "I'll only be a moment," he said once her butt was firmly planted on the barstool, and then disappeared into another room. He returned seconds later, carrying a shoebox-sized ornate case.

He set it on the counter top and opened it. She

was dying to see inside, but the contents were blocked by the open lid. When he pulled out what looked like a huge ice-pick she felt her eyes nearly fall out their sockets, her eyelids too wide to contain them.

"It's only to prick the skin."

"Why—?"

"You are descended from Élise Cantrelle, correct?"

She nodded, her eyelids refusing to relax.

"Your blood is then a personal effect of hers, as your blood comes from her blood."

"I don't understand..."

"This is just a theory, but a drop of blood placed on your crystal might just strengthen its power to call to your spirit, aka Élise Cantrelle. Much like if you had a personal effect."

"You really think that will work?"

"I have no idea," he admitted. "But blood is a powerful fluid. And I've seen stranger."

She didn't doubt that for a second.

She didn't have to think about it for long. Anything that might help uncover answers she was ready to do. She held out her left hand, first finger extended, mindful of her bandages. If Armand noticed he didn't say anything.

With gentle fingers he clasped hers. "The tools have all been sterilized," he told her. "You needn't worry; I'm very skilled at this."

Another *fact* she didn't doubt.

He quickly pricked her finger and set the ice pick aside. He then massaged the digit, much like the nurses did whenever Lottie gave blood, until a large crimson drop bubbled at the top. "Rub that on the Apophyllite. I'll grab you a bandage."

"That's it?"

"That's it. If it even works. I really don't know if it will."

Easy enough.

Carefully, she smeared the blood onto the crystal pendant. Armand held out a band-aid and just as she was getting ready to take it, it hit her. All at once, like a steamroller, the vision flattened her, demanding every ounce of her attention. Armand was gone, the modern decor of his apartment gone. All she could see was what Élise wanted her to see.

Shoving past Slade and then his brother, Xavier had to resist the urge to slap the smirk off Julien's face as he passed.

"Come with me."

"Aye, Captain."

He didn't bother to check to see if Julien followed. Rage kept his feet marching forward until he was out on the sidewalk. He was afraid if he had to look at Julien, he wouldn't be able to keep from throttling him.

"I don't know what the hell is going on with you, but you are treading on dangerous ground right now."

"Sorry little bro."

Xavier turned, fully expecting the apology to continue. He wasn't sure if he was going to be able to let it go just like that, but he would at least hear Julien out.

"But you are in my way."

The blow came hard and fast and slammed into the right side of Xavier's face. Dazed, his head swimming in and out of inky darkness, he staggered back, reaching for the support of the wall. Julien lunged at him, shoving him back with the force of a linebacker. The back of his head hit the brick.

A shot of pain, a lot of darkness, and then nothing.

Still feeling flushed, the room around her spun into a blur of indistinguishable colors. Colors she couldn't separate from the emotions twirling around her heart. She touched the empty spot on the bed beside her, still warm from Laurent's body and couldn't help the smile that spread through her entire body.

A soft knocking on the door made her scramble for her chemise. She had just slipped the fabric over her head when Rosette, grinning from ear to ear, opened the door.

"Monsieur Villere has been escorted out."

"Thank you, Rosette."

The maid lingered in the door, looking like she might burst at any moment. It was as if Élise's happiness was so enormous, it had overflowed and spilled onto the other woman.

Knowing she'd be unable to contain it for much longer, she gestured for Rosette to enter. She bounded into the room, grasping Élise's hands.

"I know I shouldn't ask..."

"No, you shouldn't."

"But?"

Élise knew her grin matched Rosette's. "He is the most amazing man."

"I'm aware of that. What kind of lover is he?"

"Rosette!"

"It's a valid question."

"It's an inappropriate question."

"I know. So...?" Rosette pressed.

Élise bit her lip and then sighed.

Rosette laughed. "I knew it! Are you going to entertain him again?"

"Yes. Tomorrow." Squeezing Rosette's hands, Élise forced her smile to drop and gave the maid a serious look. "It must stay discrete, you know that right?"

"I'm no fool."

A boom, like the crack of thunder, shattered the air. They both looked around startled.

"What was that?"

Élise shook her head just as another boom sounded. "It sounds like cannon fire." She'd heard it during the war. She'd never forget the sound.

A sudden pit formed in her stomach. Nothing good came from that noise.

Releasing Rosette, she grabbed her robe. "Go to the children. I'm going to investigate."

"Lottie." Someone patted her cheek. "Lottie Boyd."

She blinked a few times, trying to put her brain back into her skull. At that moment it was floating somewhere above her, lost in the transition between Élise's world and the present. Her eyes slowly opened and the vampire Armand's face slowly came into view.

"Are you all right?"

"Um…"

"Here, let me help you up."

He slowly eased her to a sitting position. The

modern décor of his apartment churned in a swirl of nauseating colors and textures.

"Where's Xavier?" She didn't bother asking what had happened. The bump on the back of her head and the askew barstool told her everything she needed to know.

"He never made it up here."

Fear flushed the dizziness from her head. He'd left with Julien, who was very obviously not right. He didn't even seem like the same man she'd first met in the store. Evil, cruel, filled with hatred.

She didn't trust him for a second. Not even with his own brother.

"I've got to go." She pushed to her feet.

"You might want to take it easy for a minute. I can check on Xavier."

She was pretty sure her brain was rattling around in her head as she shook it. At least that's how it felt. "I got it," she said, heading for the stairs.

Maybe she should have taken Armand up on his offer, but that same urgent tug pulled her down the stairs, out of the bar, into the courtyard, and right into Julien Villere. His grin was terrifying.

Swallowing the panic, she said lightly, "Hey. Where's Xavier?" She took a step backward but he mirrored her, maintaining their uncomfortably close proximity to each other.

"That's nothing you need to worry about. In fact, you should forget about him, about this city. We don't like you here."

We?

If she was frightened of him before, she was terrified of him now. His expression, his eyes, the tone of his words…evil, just evil.

She took another step back and he again took one

forward. His body language was definitely threatening and even though he wasn't touching her, she felt trapped. He was so close, if she tried to run he could easily stop her. She had no doubt he would.

"Is he okay?"

"He'll live."

Oh God. Xavier. What had Julien done?

She had to get away. She had to find Xavier.

She was going to run. Maybe if she just bolted, she'd take him by surprise. And if he grabbed her she'd fight with every ounce of strength in her body. Aim for his balls, eyes, anything that looked soft and painful. She'd claw, bite, and kick if she had to. She just needed to run.

"What are you doing?"

It was Armand. He'd appeared out of nowhere and stood a menacing few inches from Julien. In the dim light of the courtyard he looked positively terrifying.

"You are not welcome here, Julien Villere," Armand enunciated the name like it a threat. "I assumed that was obvious."

Julien swallowed. She was shocked to see the fear in his eyes. She took the opportunity to move away. He didn't follow this time, clearly locked in place by the vampire's hard stare.

"I—"

"No. You will not speak. You will not make excuses. You will leave. Not just my property but you will also leave Miss Boyd alone. Is that understood?"

He nodded.

"Say, 'yes'."

"Yes."

"Good."

Lottie decided she'd watched enough. She slipped

from the courtyard and down the narrow alley. When she emerged onto the sidewalk, her breath was once again sucked from her lungs. Slumped next to the building wall, like a homeless man passed out on the street, was Xavier, blood dripping from his nose.

"Oh my God!" She was in the process of kneeling over him, when just like before, the vision hit her, knocking her out of the present and into the past.

CHAPTER EIGHTEEN

*T*he panic in Élise's gut had spread to her chest by the time she reached the front door, squeezing her heart tight. There was no hesitation in her hand as it grasped the knob and turned.

What greeted her stole her breath. Lying in the street was Laurent, blood seeping from his chest.

"No!" She ran over to him, kneeling on the ground beside him. "Oh God." His shirt was already soaked through with red. "Oh God no. No, no, no, no, no, no."

What should she do? How could she stop this? Gingerly she touched his shirt. There was too much blood. It was beginning to spill onto the ground.

"No." It was a useless wail and she knew it. His wounds were too severe.

Gently, she touched his face. His lids slowly lifted. For a brief moment her heart lightened and then she saw his eyes. Those beautiful black irises were dull, the light behind them, so recently emblazoned with passion, dim.

"Élise...Mon amour..." His hand rose, slow and unsteady, to touch her face. She clasped his hand

tightly to her cheek. "My beautiful love," he whispered, the words choked. "I am so sorry."

Shaking her head, she closed her eyes against the tears pouring from them. There had to be something...

"Élise, please look at me." His voice was weak. She obeyed, but her entire body trembled with the effort. To look at him was to accept his fate. "Given the chance, I wouldn't take anything back. I only regret...my son...and that I won't be able to love you for a lifetime."

"Please, Laurent, don't..."

But at once she knew her pleas went unheard. The remainder of the dim light drained from his eyes as the life oozed from his body.

It was hardly the first time she experienced death, but this was different. It felt like her soul was torn from her body as his soul escaped his. She didn't think she could bear the pain. Her body shuddered as every piece of happiness, every ounce of hope she'd dared to dream died on the street with him.

Lottie woke up sobbing. Her insides were broken, twisted into a million knots that tortured her guts. Élise's pain devoured her...devastated her...consumed her. She couldn't think, could barely breathe. It was a good thing her heart beat automatically or she'd be dead.

"Lottie?"

The warmth below her stirred. She couldn't see who, or what, she lay on. She could only sob harder.

Strong arms encircled her body. "Ssshhh, I know." Lips pressed to her head.

Voice recognition finally kicked in. Xavier...she

was in Xavier's arms. She wanted to be happy he was okay, wanted to rejoice at his gentle touch, but could only sob, burying her face in his firm, muscular chest.

Keeping her cradled tightly in his arms, he sat up. She remembered—they must have been lying on the sidewalk. And now they sat on the sidewalk, her crying uncontrollably, and him holding her.

"I know," he murmured again, squeezing her tight.

If only she could speak, she would thank him, express her eternal gratitude for him. But there were no words she could utter, only unending, overpowering sorrow.

Xavier was pretty sure his heart was being chipped away with every choked sob, every shudder of Lottie's body. He'd do anything to take away her pain. Anything.

All he could do now was hold her. Hopefully, it offered some comfort. He knew what she ached for though, and knew he would never be enough. He would never be his grandfather.

Oops, there went another piece of his heart.

It didn't matter. Right now, only one thing mattered.

He stroked the silky strands of her hair, momentarily smoothing the wild curls. Her sobs were getting quieter but he was in no rush. As long as it took...

It was the first time since he'd come to that he was able to process everything that had happened. First, Julien was getting his ass kicked so hard whatever craziness possessed him would be expelled.

He had never been violent toward his brother, but at that moment, he was ready to tear the bastard's arms off.

Second, living Laurent's death had been intense. And he'd thought experiencing the night with Élise was heavy. The *memory* had hit him right after Julien rammed his head into the wall. It must have to do something with the gifts they'd doused on the altar before leaving the house, and that Julien happened to knock him out right where Laurent had been shot.

The only reason he wasn't taking Laurent's death as hard as Lottie was because he'd been having dreams about his grandfather for years, even if he hadn't realized it at the time. This might have been a little less "uplifting" than the other dreams he'd had, but Xavier was more pissed than anything. If he could find the grave of the southern bigot who'd shot Laurent he'd piss on it.

Which wouldn't be enough but it'd make him feel better. Somewhat.

Her sobs had eased to muted whimpers with the occasional shudder breath thrown in. It wasn't perfect but it'd have to do.

"Lottie," he said quietly. "I'm going take you home, okay?" He meant the Villere Guest House, of course, but saying "home" felt so much more natural.

She nodded into his chest.

The position was awkward and it took a little bit of contortion on his part and his head throbbed with every movement, but he was able to get to his feet still cradling her.

Her cries had subsided and now she was perfectly still, too still. She remained that way the entire walk back. Almost like she was comatose. He didn't prefer the crying, but at least then he knew she was working through the emotions that came with Élise's memories. Now she just seemed numb.

He had no desire to go through the house—there wasn't a single person in his family he wanted to run into, except strangely enough, his mother might not be too bad. He still wasn't interested in explaining anything, so he headed for the side alley instead.

As he walked past the front of the store, something caught his eye—a bright, flickering light coming from behind the shutters.

"What the hell?" Peering through the shutter cracks confirmed his suspicion. Sanite's altar had been restored, complete with dozens of lit candles. There might be even more candles than before.

He'd have to take care of that, but not until Lottie was safely in the suite. Assuming the fowl feet did indeed offer protection as they seemed to.

He was still coming to grips with the idea that his great-great-great...aunt was threatening the woman in his arms. He still wasn't sure why though. Other than being related to Élise Cantrelle, Sanite Villere had no reason to hate Lottie. He understood why she might not care for Élise, since, according to his recurring dream, Sanite hadn't exactly been keen on Laurent hooking up with Élise in the first place. And then when it did happen, he was shot and killed.

But could Sanite really blame Élise? And why would she hate Lottie, who had absolutely nothing to do with any of it?

Women...

Lottie remained completely still even as he set her on the bed—staring off into the distance. It was not only beginning to worry him, he was beginning to become irritated by the situation, which in turn made him irritated with himself. He knew it was only

207

jealousy fueling his angst, but that didn't make it any better.

"I'm going to run you a bath," he told her. Hopefully that would snap her out of her daze. Or make her feel better, or both.

Was it possible she wasn't exactly herself? Like Julien wasn't exactly himself? Pausing in the bathroom door he glanced back at her. Still sitting against the mass of pillows piled in front of the headboard, still staring into the distance, her beautiful face still troubled.

He had to wonder if it was actually Lottie on the bed, or Élise.

The chicken feet dangled from the shower-head, their painted toes curled and twisted. He plugged the tub and started the water. Right before leaving he covered the feet with a hand towel. He didn't dare remove them, but Lottie didn't need to look at that while relaxing in a bath.

She hadn't changed position, not even a millimeter. He sat on the bed at her feet and said her name. She grimaced but didn't move. "Hey. I got the water running." Nothing. He started removing her shoes. "Well, I guess if you won't take off your clothes, I'll have to."

Finally her eyes flicked to his. With a grin, he set her shoes aside and rested his hand on her smooth ankle. "Are you back?" he asked.

She didn't give him much warning. She stared at him for a brief minute, her eyes scanning his face, before leaning forward and pressing her lips to his.

What started as a soft kiss quickly became a deep kiss, and then her hands wrapped around his head and she was on her knees, body pressed close.

It wasn't—he didn't—he shouldn't—he couldn't

stop...

Was it him she kissed? Or Laurent? Was she acting as Élise or herself? He had no idea.

One hand gripped her close and the other kept her just far enough away that her groin wasn't pressed to him. "Lottie," he gasped between kisses. "I don't know—"

Her tongue, firm yet sweet, slid into his mouth and he forgot what he didn't know. Or that he probably shouldn't be taking advantage of her vulnerability.

She managed to snake her body closer and her hand under his shirt. Between her hands all over his flesh, her hips undulating slowly against him, and her fiery kiss, he forgot everything that wasn't her.

Especially when she yanked off his shirt and her lips found their way to his neck, then his chest, then his stomach. When her fingers found the waistband of his jeans, his brain clicked back on. He wanted this, wanted her, but he needed to know she felt the same. That she wasn't just reaching to him to have a piece of Laurent.

He started to stop her. Placing his hands on her shoulders, he was prepared to gently push her back when she moaned. "God, Xavier. I want you so much. I need you." Her blue eyes flicked up. "In my mouth. In me."

Well, there went the last bit of his brain attempting to hold out.

Which was good because his pants were unbuckled and Lottie's mouth was all over his cock. Good because making any decisions that didn't revolve around pleasure weren't even on the table at this point.

But shit, he was going to come if she didn't stop.

"Lottie," he breathed her name.

She seemed to increase her efforts. She added a hand in addition to her mouth, sliding up and down his shaft with perfect rhythm.

"Lottie, please."

Her other hand cupped his balls and that was it. This time when he said her name, it came out with a moan. He couldn't stop the wall of pleasure that burst through him and she seemed to welcome it, taking him deep inside her mouth.

When the last wave of pleasure shuddered through his body, she pulled back, delicately wiping the corners of her mouth. She glanced up at him, her big blue eyes sparkling, and grinned.

That snapped him out of his post-orgasm coma. There were still so many things he wanted to do to her.

Guiding her up until she was mostly eye-level, he wrapped her lips in a soft, warm kiss that quickly escalated into a heady, deep kiss. He could taste the sex on her tongue and that only excited him more. Soon enough it would be her sex he tasted.

She pulled back, coyly pulling off her cotton dress and then unhooking her bra. She bit her lip as she slid the bra straps from her shoulders. The moment her hands were free, he dove in for another kiss. She eased back onto the mattress and he followed, keeping her mouth firmly embraced by his.

It was his turn to explore her body. Starting with her neck and earlobes, trailing over her collarbones, down to her perfectly sized breasts and erect pink nipples. She moaned and arched into him. Fuck, with the noises she made just by him teasing her nipples, he couldn't wait to hear her come.

He stayed at her breasts for a while—thoroughly

enjoying the way she squirmed as his tongue circled her nipples—before heading south, pausing briefly to enjoy her delicately curved, perfectly feminine belly.

Her panties came off with a quick tug. There was no resistance in her muscles as he pushed her legs wide, exposing the delicate pink skin of her sex, glistening and just waiting for his tongue.

Fuck, she tasted better than he imagined, and the way she moaned and twisted her hips as he lapped her clit and dipped in, out, and around, made him just want to devour her more.

She cried out as she came, shoving her hips into him. He loved it, savoring every last drop of her orgasm.

His cock was rock hard again. As much as he'd love to be inside her, he wasn't sure that desire was mutual. But as he rose from the glorious valley that was the space between her thighs, she reached forward and gently grabbed his member, guiding it into her smooth slick depths.

He about lost his ever-loving mind. Especially when she moaned his name.

She wrapped her legs around his waist, pulling him deep inside as she ground her hips into him.

He closed his eyes. Jesus, the feel of her sweet, warm sex, the feel of her soft body rocking beneath him, the feel of her.

"Xavier. Look at me."

He did. One look into those gorgeous blue orbs was all it took. He groaned as his orgasm started to release.

"Kiss me. Please. I need you to kiss me as you come."

Gladly.

The minute his lips touched hers, she tightened

211

her thigh hold on him and, locking her fingers in his hair, pulled him as close as possible. She whimpered under his kiss and he felt the muscles of her core clench tight as her orgasm joined his.

It lasted longer than it should and left him weak, a little bit drained, and 100% satiated. Propping onto his elbows so that the bulk of his weight was supported, he looked at her and grinned. She started to smile and then frowned.

Shit.

"Oh! Shit!"

He jumped up and ran to the bathroom, shutting off the water, the level lapping dangerously close to the edge. The overflow drain was working overtime trying to keep up.

"Good thing I decided to splurge on the oversized tub and the water pressure sucks," he said, emerging from the bathroom. "Otherwise we might have had a mess on our hands—"

He stopped short when he caught sight of her. Back to sitting, sheet wrapped tight around her, knees pulled to chest, looking...morose.

Well, didn't that just drive a knife into his gut.

"What's wrong?" He didn't really need to ask; he had a pretty good what was upsetting her, but it was a good way to fill the awkward silence.

Of course she just shook her head.

It was one thing to have the woman you love—shit...wait...what?—pine for another man, it was another when that man was your long deceased grandfather. And to have the best sex of your life tainted by that knowledge was not a pleasant realization.

"He didn't die in your arms."

Her head shot up.

"What?"

"Laurent. He didn't die in your arms."

"He may as well have." She shook her head again. "You wouldn't understand."

"Wouldn't I? I was there too. I got to live the whole thing...when my dickhead brother knocked me out. Leaving Élise's and feeling pretty damn good," the same way he'd felt moments ago, "getting confronted by some jealous southern dude, probably from Georgia judging from his accent, getting called a monkey half-breed, and then getting shot. And then the very unpleasant experience of dying in the street, and having to see the woman you just fell in love with watch you die—knowing there's nothing you can do to ease her heartbreak and feeling like a coward because you couldn't prevent it. Yeah, I think I understand just fine."

She just stared at him for a while and for a moment he thought based on her expression maybe he was wrong. Maybe she was just processing Élise's grief and her unhappiness had nothing to do with him. Maybe she really wanted to tell him how much he meant to her and with everything that had happened didn't know how.

"Wait, did you say Georgia?"

Or maybe not.

He swallowed what was left of his pride. "That's what the accent sounded like to me."

"What did he look like?"

He started to describe the man but she didn't give him the chance.

"Thirties, brown hair, yellow teeth? Like, smoked-three-packs-a-day yellow?"

"Well, he wasn't exactly smiling at Laurent so I didn't see his teeth but yeah, sounds about right."

"Henry..." Her eyes went distant again and then teared up.

Seeing those blue orbs gloss over with sadness made him want to reach for her, to comfort her. He refrained.

Her gaze snapped to him. "We can't tell Élise. It would kill her to know. She was supposed to dine with Henry that evening. She blew it off to be with Laurent."

"We can't tell Élise anything. She's dead."

Lottie buried her face in her hands. For a minute he thought just the mention of her dead relative was enough to send her over the edge. But then she rose up. "God, you're right. This is messing with my head big time."

"There is a nice hot bath waiting for you." He gestured toward the bathroom. "I hear many people find them soothing."

Her expression turned wistful. "I could definitely stand to clean up." Her gaze shot to him. "I mean—"

He held up his hand to stop her. He didn't want to hear any more. "Hey, I'm going to dig up some grub."

From wistful to shameful, she was a woman of constantly changing emotions. "Sure."

Perfect. He had to get out of there. He knew he'd need to deal with what had happened between them at some point, but right now there were other, more pressing issues. Namely, his crazy fucking family.

"Be right back," he said to Lottie without looking at her.

Within seconds he'd made his escape only to linger in the sitting room. Should he be leaving her alone? In a tub filled with water? What if she blacked out again?

He looked toward the bedroom door.

God, if he went back in there now he'd seem like the biggest creep. She hadn't had any problems with water since he hung the chicken feet, so maybe they were doing their job.

He'd have to chance it.

Ten minutes. He could be back in ten minutes. Not only did he need to clear his own messed-up head—which was a big part of it—but he also needed to dismantle Sanite's altar and then find Julien and beat his ass. Not necessarily in that order.

CHAPTER NINETEEN

Lottie was a mess of tattered, conflicted emotions as she watched Xavier scurry from the room. She wasn't lying when she said her head was screwed. Her brain was pretty much scrambled eggs at that point.

What the hell was wrong with her? How could she seduce Xavier, knowing what Élise had experienced? How could she put her own pleasure above the tragedy of her great-grandmother? Just because she, Lottie, had made the sudden realization that life was short and she should seize the moment didn't mean she should disrespect the memory of her ancestor.

But she had. And in the dirtiest possible way.

And it was so good. He felt so good. Touching him, being with him, under him… everything was so perfect. He was perfect.

God, but every time she thought about the amazing experience of being with him, she was reminded of Élise's tragic love affair. How could she revel in her own happiness when Élise's had been stolen?

Emotionally shattered and unable to comprehend

everything that had happened, she grabbed her
sleeping tank and shorts, and made her way to the
bathroom. How sweet of Xavier to draw her a bath. It
was just one of many sweet gestures he'd made in the
last several days. Gestures she had no idea how to
repay. Gestures she didn't feel she deserved.

The water was still hot enough it stung a little as
she stepped into the tub. It was a good sting, but she
still had to ease into it. With a sigh, she leaned back
against the porcelain and let her mind go blank.

She was only able to enjoy a few moments of
silence. The shrieking ripped through her eardrums
before the memory hit her. Like the cries of a feral
animal, it assaulted her with despair, anger, and
horror.

*Élise's head jerked up. Too drained to cry any
more, too exhausted to move, she'd stayed with
Laurent's body for what seemed like a very long time.*

*The inhuman sounds came from a Creole woman,
the same woman from the courtyard where she'd spied
on the Voodoo ceremony...where she'd first run into
Laurent.*

*The woman's face was twisted in anguish,
contorted into features that seemed better suited to an
underworld demon than a young woman. Her black
eyes, the same impossibly dark eyes Laurent had,
were filled with pure, vile hatred.*

*With little warning, she lunged at Élise with all
the ferocity of a wild animal. She jumped back and the
woman cowered over Laurent.*

"What did you do?" she hissed between wails.

*"Nothing." With startled steps, Élise backed
away.*

"You killed him! You killed my brother!"

"No! I..."

The woman jumped up. "I told him to stay away from you! I told him he had no business with a white woman! He didn't listen and now look!"

"I didn't..." She didn't what? Know their affair might cause trouble? Of course she knew. But she never dreamt...

"I should kill you," the woman said, her voice filled with venom. "A life for a life." Her expression turned hard. "I will kill you."

There was nothing but truth in her words. And there was no doubt in Élise's mind she intended to follow through with her promise.

"I curse you. Even in death you will have no rest. Your kin will know no peace. As you have ruined my family so shall yours. You will walk this earth until the blood of your blood is spilled upon your grave."

In an instant, everything changed. Despite her thundering heart, all Élise could think about were her children. Of course she feared for her life, but she feared more for theirs. Though it was tempting to run back into the house, to bar the doors and latch the shutters, she didn't dare. To do so would be leading a wolf into the chicken coop.

As the woman lunged again, hands outstretched like claws, she turned the other direction and ran. Ran in a way she hadn't run since she was a child. The woman—Laurent's sister—followed, cursing and screaming. Some words she recognized. Some she did not.

She ran without a destination in mind. Her mind a blur of fear, regret, and sadness. Shrouded by grief, the streets were no longer familiar.

The longer she ran, the more frenzied her enemy became. Shouts became screeches. Threats became more powerful, more intense. She kept repeating over and over, "You will not rest until the blood of your blood is spilled upon your grave!"

Élise didn't know what it meant, but she knew to be frightened. There was no escape, no way to flee the enemy. Her lungs burned, her sight unfocused, her slippers long discarded, her bare feet were bloody. Fear and the desire to protect her children kept her moving.

A thick fog had settled over the city, making navigation even more challenging. She made a quick left and then a right, hoping to lose the still screaming woman in the fog. It didn't work.

Ahead, she could hear the lapping water of the Mississippi River kissing its muddy banks. The fog would be thickest there. On the docks, she might be able to hide in it. At least confuse the woman enough to escape home.

The wood was rough under her already damaged feet. Splintered and uneven, it dug mercilessly into her flesh.

Still, she pressed on. Running down the dock until she came across some large shipping barrels, barely shadows in the dense fog. She could no longer see her enemy, but she could hear her. With attempted stealth, she slipped between two barrels and went still.

She heard the woman slow her chase and then pause. "You think you can hide from me?" she cackled. "I will haunt you in life. I will haunt you in death."

Élise wanted to plead with her, beg for understanding and forgiveness, but she was pretty sure she'd receive neither. Laurent's sister was crazy with grief. And she could not blame her for that. Had she not three wonderful children to think of, she could easily succumb to her own sadness.

"Do you know what you've done?" the woman asked. Despair once again filled her voice and it cracked with tears. "You've taken everything from me. Laurent wasn't just my brother, he was my entire family, my life. But you stole that! You stole him! And you robbed a son of his father. Wasn't it enough he saved your child? You had to have more of him. You had to seduce him. Prey on his weakness as a man. When you know you had no business with him. That white men don't take kindly to their women mixing."

Élise bit her lip. God, she was right. Laurent's sister was right. She truly hadn't meant anything by it though. She just...wanted to...love him. And be loved by him.

Two things in this world that should never be wrong.

But they were—at least they were in the world she lived in. And she knew it.

She closed her eyes, fresh tears sliding down her cheeks. What had she done? And how could she fix it?

Out of the mist, Laurent's sister's face suddenly appeared, inches from hers.

"And you will be punished."

Élise screamed, jumping backward. Her feet skimmed the edge of the dock, toes barely on the edge, and she flailed desperately to keep her balance. Her swinging arms weren't enough to stall her momentum and keep her on the dock. As she fell backward, her head hit something hard, pain and blackness shooting through her just as the cold, Mississippi water saturated her skin.

Darkness began to engulf her as liquid seared her lungs, choking out her breath. Her last thoughts were of her children and the man she'd never meant to kill.

Lottie woke up gagging on water. Submerged, she shot up in the bathtub, coughing and gasping for air.

"Oh my God," she rasped.

Suddenly she knew. She knew exactly what Élise was trying to tell her.

Even in death you will have no rest. Your kin will know no peace. As you have ruined my family so shall yours. You will walk this earth until the blood of your blood is spilled upon your grave.

She was trapped. Cursed by Sanite Villere to walk this earth. Separated from her family, from Laurent...

Blood of your blood.

Lottie was the blood.

Without drying off, she threw on her sleep tank and shorts. After grabbing a knife from the kitchenette, she slipped into her flip-flops and ran out of the Guest House suite. Unlike Élise's final run through New Orleans though, Lottie knew exactly where she headed.

CHAPTER TWENTY

From the kitchen window, Xavier stared in disbelief at Lottie dashing through the courtyard. Hair soaking wet and dripping, wearing a barely there tank top and flimsy shorts, and running like her life depending on it.

The butter knife he was washing fell into the sink with a clank. "What the hell?"

He half expected to see Julien chasing after her. Not that he'd seen that slimy bastard—and he'd looked—since they returned. Or even some fucked up apparition of his long deceased aunt. But there was nothing. Only Lottie.

Forgetting the half-made sandwiches on the counter and barely taking time to turn off the faucet, he sprinted through the house, the shop, and out the front door just in time to glimpse her disappearing around the corner.

He took off after her. Man, she was booking it and he had to push his legs to keep up with her, let alone try to catch her. He'd barely narrowed the distance between them when she reached Rampart. He hoped the traffic on the busy street would slow her down, but she just kept running. He wasn't even sure she looked.

"Fuck!"

Whatever mission she was on, she was *on* it. At least he had a pretty good idea where she was headed.

Ducking around cars and ignoring the blaring horns, he continued after her. Just as he expected, she went directly for the locked gate to St. Louis Cemetery Number One.

For a brief second he thought he might be able to catch her as she climbed, but she scaled the gate like a champ. She didn't even climb down the other side. She jumped.

Holy. Shit. When that girl wanted something…

But he knew that all too well.

He climbed over the gate with ease but that's where the *easy* part stopped. She was nowhere in sight, he had no idea where she might be going, and the cemetery was a confusing jumble of crumbling tombs. He called her name and as he expected, didn't get a response.

Well, good thing he liked to run, because it looked like he was going to be doing a lot of it.

Lottie was able to run directly to Élise's grave. Without hesitation. Without thinking. Like she'd been visiting it daily for her entire life.

That all changed when she reached it. She'd been so driven to get there, she hadn't thought about what she was going to do. But now that she stood feet from the tomb, she couldn't act. The knife hung uselessly in her hand.

She knew what she needed to do, knew there was

no other way.

Until the blood of your blood is spilled upon your grave.

She was the last of Élise's blood. The lone survivor of centuries of untimely deaths and horrible *accidents*. And she knew what "spilled blood" meant.

Thing was, she wasn't suicidal. Not even remotely. And the prospect of slitting her own wrist made her heart buck and her stomach knot. She'd hoped it would be easy, that she would arrive at the grave and the same thing that happened nights ago would happen again. Possession, wrist slit, end of story. But there was nothing. Not even that familiar tug urging her forward.

"What am I supposed to do?" she asked the grave. "Why won't you help me?"

Only unnatural silence greeted her. No sounds of cars whizzing by on the busy street at the front of the cemetery walls, no birds, not even the flutter of wind.

"Please! Help me!"

More silence. Surely Sanite was interfering. Preventing Élise from helping her...

Why couldn't she do this? If she didn't spill her blood on Élise's grave, then what? Élise remained trapped, tortured to walk this earth, separated from her children, from Laurent, unable to find peace? And what would happen to her? Sanite Villere would stop at nothing to keep punishing Élise. Wouldn't Lottie suffer the same fate as her parents, and so many others before her? Doomed to die some unnatural way...

She tried to think of the good that would come of her death. She could see her parents. She could know Élise and Laurent, see their love. She could be with Amélie, Jean Michel, Matthieu. She'd never be alone again.

But what about Xavier?

She pushed him from her mind. There was no time for that. She needed to act. Now.

Ripping the bandages from her wrist, she tossed them aside. Her hand shook violently when she lifted the knife and pressed it to the raw marks. Taking a deep breath, she tried to calm her mind, her body. She could do this. She would do this.

She heard a crack and felt something fall to the ground. Blade still pressed to her wrist, she glanced down. The evil eye lay broken at her feet. Shattered in two, it simply dropped from her necklace.

"What the—"

"Here. Let me help with that." The knife was suddenly yanked from her hands. Strong arms wrapped around her chest and drug her back away from the grave.

She screamed. She recognized that voice.

The blade found its way to her neck. "If you really want to die, I'm more than happy to help," Julien murmured into her ear. "But I can't let you free my prisoner. Élise is mine. For eternity."

Pain seared through her as the blade slid across her neck.

CHAPTER TWENTY-ONE

Xavier felt like he was running in circles and gaining nothing but a shirt saturated with sweat. He'd run every aisle, checked every corner, and still no Lottie. The cemetery wasn't even that fucking big!

And then he heard her scream.

Shit, she was less than fifty feet away.

Scrambling through two narrow tombs and over one that had been reduced to a pile of bricks, he emerged on a walkway and into a scene out of a horror movie. Julien had Lottie restrained, gripping her tightly across the chest, and what looked like a knife pressed to her throat.

Closing the distance between them with superhuman speed, he yanked his brother back and flung him to the ground. The knife went flying and Lottie fell to the ground clutching her neck. Where he could see blood, lots of blood, seeping through her fingers and onto the ground.

Blood that immediately blurred his vision and fueled his fists. He could see nothing but hatred when he looked at his brother attempting to regain his feet. Lifting him off the ground using his hair as a handle,

Xavier twisted him around and clocked him twice in the face, splitting his lip and probably breaking his nose.

If it hadn't been for Lottie bleeding behind him, he probably would have kept pounding his brother's face until it was no longer recognizable. Luckily for Julien, his eyes rolled back in his head and he went limp. Xavier dropped him like a rag doll and rushed to her.

Still clutching her neck, she was searching for something. Desperately, from her body language. Staring at the ground like she'd lost a contact, she kicked at the crushed shell and dirt paths, flicking back and forth like a penned coyote.

"Lottie...Lottie." He grabbed her elbow. "Lottie!"

Her eyes were wild when she looked at him. "I have to find it."

"What?"

"The knife! I need it!" Tears glistened her eyes. "I need it." And then she began to cry.

He pulled her into his arms where she sobbed into his chest. "Oh God, please. Please Lottie, don't do this to me." He hugged her tightly for a moment before taking her shoulder he moved her back. Her entire body trembled and she looked at him with fear and desperation in her eyes. "Please, talk to me. Tell me what's going on. But first let me see your neck."

"I know what Élise has been trying to tell me," she said through tears. "She's cursed, Xavier. Sanite Villere cursed her. And my family. She blames Élise for Laurent's death. Sanite found him in the street, after..." She swallowed a sob. "She was furious with Élise. Cursing and threatening to kill her, she chased her to the river. Where...she drowned. Élise hit her head and drowned. I think that's why the weird things keep happening in the bathroom. It has to do with the water. Like it gave her power or something."

As she spoke, he gently peeled her fingers away and took inventory of the gash on her neck. It was bleeding like a bitch, but not that big and nowhere near her jugular—thank God. She'd definitely need stitches though. He replaced her hand with his, applying gentle pressure to the wound.

"And until the blood of her blood is spilled on her grave, she'll never know peace. She's trapped here. Trapped here until..." In a flash, the fear and desperation were replaced with determination. "That's why I need the knife."

He felt his eyes narrow. "For what?"

She pressed her lips together. "I'm the last of the blood. Blood of her blood must be spilled..."

"Oh, no. I don't think so. If you're thinking what I think you're thinking—no. Hell no. Fuck no."

"It's the only way."

"Killing yourself?" He couldn't believe what he was hearing. But it didn't matter if he believed it or not, he wasn't letting it happen.

"I have to. Believe me I don't want to, but I can't leave her trapped. Away from her family, from Laurent. If I do it, the curse is broken. Not just for Élise, but for me, my family, my descendents."

"You won't have any fucking descendents if you kill yourself," he said bitterly. "Besides, how do you know it'll even work?"

She held out her left hand, wrist upturned. The jagged pink marks from her earlier run-in with a nail file stood out brightly against her light skin. "That's what Élise was trying to tell me the first time I was here. I didn't listen. So she had to tell me her story so I would."

"I..." He frowned. "Let's think about this for a moment, okay?" He tossed a quick glance in Julien's direction to make sure the bastard was still knocked out. He was. "Tell me exactly what Sanite said when she cursed Élise?"

She swallowed, the movement of her throat working against his hand. A hand that was wet with her blood. He really needed to get her to a doctor.

"Even in death you will have no rest. Your kin will know no peace. As you have ruined my family so shall yours. You will walk this earth until the blood of your blood is spilled upon your grave," she repeated the words like it was the Pledge of Allegiance. Like she'd done it a hundred times. He imagined in her mind she had.

"Why do you think that means you need to kill yourself?"

She gave him a hard look. "I think we all know what spilling blood means."

If the situation wasn't so serious, her *you idiot* tone would have made him smile.

"Well growing up with the women in my family I know a little something about curses. They're rarely figurative."

"What else can spilling blood mean?"

"I have an idea. Which one is Élise's grave?"

She pointed to one of the tombs.

The wind began to pick up and Xavier had a sneaking suspicion it wasn't because there was a cold front moving in.

"I think we'd better hurry," he said. Reluctantly removing his own hand, he took her hand and placed it over the still bleeding wound. He should have torn off a piece of his shirt. There was blood everywhere. Too late now.

"Put pressure on this," he told her as the wind kicked up a notch, whistling through the tombs and tossing Lottie's hair around wildly.

Once he was satisfied she'd protected her neck enough, he took her free hand and they ran for the grave in half-crouched positions. The wind now whipped violently through the cemetery, sending dust and dirt and trash flying past.

Yanking open the gate to the short, spiked wrought iron fence protecting the tomb, he pulled her in and guided her to the narrow spot between the side of the concrete wall and the fence edge safely out of the wind. Squatting, she backed up as he squeezed in beside her.

The wind was so loud it screeched. Ripping the sleeve from his Tee, he placed it over the still bleeding cut. He really should have done it right away. But at least there was enough blood for his plan. "Hold this."

"What are you thinking?" she shouted.

He took her hand, the one covered in her own blood, and placed it on the tomb. "I think your spilled blood is just that. Your blood...spilled on Elise's grave...like merely touching it."

She stared at him like he was crazy but sure enough, the moment the red of her blood stained the white concrete, light exploded around them. So bright, he had to turn away. He pulled her into his chest, hopefully shielding her from whatever came next.

Unless he physically plugged her ears, there was little more he could do. He hated feeling so helpless.

He glanced down to make sure she was okay. She stared upward, toward the night sky, her eyes filled with wonder and a conflicted mixture of tears, happiness, and trepidation.

Following her gaze he saw what had her so

emotional. Floating just above the top of the tomb was the shimmering image of Élise's ghost. Bathed in the bright white light, she looked every bit like he remembered. Her hair, long and curly and blond—just like Lottie's—twisted around her face like smoke. Her gauzy white gown, nearly as transparent as she was, billowed like wafts of cloud.

He also saw the source of trepidation. Swirling around Élise with tornadic fury, was an inky blackness. It twisted and coiled like an angry snake, trapping Élise within its—or he should say her—vortex.

"Good to know the women in my family don't hold grudges," he muttered.

Lottie's now frightened eyes turned to him. "Now what do we do? She's trapped."

It came to him in an instant, the repressed teachings of years of Voodoo lore.

"I have another idea!" At this point he had to scream to be heard. His fingers still damp with her blood he began to draw on the tomb wall. Even though he'd rarely paid attention to Grandmere's lectures, the design was so firmly etched in his subconscious, it just flowed from his fingers.

He hoped like hell it worked.

At first Lottie had no idea what to expect when Xavier began drawing an elaborate symbol from her blood on the side of Élise's grave. It was similar to the one engraved on her necklace, with swooping scrolls and crosses and star-like symbols, so she knew it was probably some spirit's vévé. But she had no idea whose it might be, or what to expect after it was drawn.

The moment he finished, he chanted, "Odu Legba, Papa Legba, open the door, your children are waiting. Papa Legba, open the door, your children await."

She stared at him in awe as he repeated the chant. The knowledge he possessed, knowledge he'd probably denied for years, was astounding. And his instinct to apply that knowledge...he was every bit Laurent's grandson. He just had to believe.

It seemed impossible, but both the screeching and wind increased until her ears rang and she had to clutch the fence to avoid being swept away. One arm firmly wrapped around her, one grasping the fence post next to her, Xavier yelled out the chant once again. This time with more urgency and a sense of forcefulness to his words.

The moment the last "your children await" was uttered, the world began to shake. Loose bricks from deteriorated tombs clattered to the ground. The fence creaked and groaned as hundreds of years of rust resisted the jostling. All around the chaos intensified. Between the wind and the screeching and the trembling earth...it was too much. If it hadn't been for Xavier's strong embrace, she wasn't sure she'd be able to hold it together.

Especially when a huge, vacant-eyed skull rose from the ground. In spite of everything she'd seen to date, she felt her eyes widen. She shrank back into Xavier's grasp.

The wind immediately dropped as the inky black tornado recoiled, the screeching reduced to a whimper.

"What is it?" she asked Xavier.

"Papa Legba...I assume. That's who I summoned

232

anyway. He's the gatekeeper between the spirit world and ours."

While she definitely cared, she was actually happier to see that the skull—Papa Legba—was effectively shielding the beautiful, shimmering ghost of Élise from the inky, hovering darkness. It still churned angrily, but off to the side, away from Élise. She had no doubt if Xavier's body wasn't draped over hers, its anger would be focused on her.

Slowly, the skull opened its mouth and a blinding light shot out, turning midnight into noon. She was forced to turn away for a minute until her eyes adjusted.

Xavier nudged her. "Lottie, you need to see this."

Squinting, she turned toward the light. The mouth of the skull was stretched abnormally wide, like the unhinged jaw of a snake. The light, beautiful and serene at the same time, poured from the gaping maw. When her eyes adjusted, she gasped.

"Oh! Xavier!" Standing in the light was Laurent, flanked by what could only be Amélie, Jean-Michel, Matthieu, and Nathanael.

With a smile as big as hers must be, Élise walked through the air toward them. Just before stepping into the waiting arms of Laurent and her family, she turned toward them.

"Merci, mon enfant," she said, her voice distant, like it originated somewhere far away, yet perfectly clear. She looked toward a couple that Lottie hadn't noticed before.

Her hand flew to her mouth. "Oh God!" Xavier's embrace immediately tightened. "My parents," she murmured. Standing off to the side, her father waved and her mother blew her a kiss. She barely had a chance to wave back before Élise stepped in the skull

233

and its mouth began to close.

And like that, it was over.

The inkiness that was Sanite Villere howled one final time in what sounded like frustrated anguish, and then dissipated in a rush of ice-cold air. The skull slowly sank back into the earth and the cemetery returned to quiet darkness, the faint sound of traffic buzzing in the distance.

There was nothing left to hold her together. Her organs, muscles, and bones all seemed to blend together into liquefied mush, and if it weren't for the weak shell of her skin and Xavier's strong embrace, she would have melted into a puddle right there.

She was pretty sure there were tears on her face, and she was pretty sure she was still bleeding, but she couldn't feel any of it. All she could feel was Xavier and she was so grateful for him. If only her mouth worked…

Happy, relieved, a little sad, bewildered—all emotions swirled inside her. She didn't know how to begin to process them. It had been such a chaotic ride to this point and now that it was over, she was left a jumbled mess, a shell of someone she barely remembered. Someone who existed before her parents died.

Xavier scooped her up into his arms, carefully easing from behind Élise's tomb, though the wrought iron gate, and into the aisle. "Let's get you to the hospital," he said.

She rested her head on his shoulder. He smelled so good and she lost herself in the scent, letting the memory of him above her and in her keep her grounded. She felt like she could just disappear and never return. Sleep and never wake.

A figure rose from the ground before them and in

the back recesses of her mind she realized it was Julien and that she should probably be afraid. But with Xavier's protective arms around her, fear didn't fit into her muddled emotions.

Xavier didn't slow on his approach and by the time they reached him, Julien was standing and dusting off his pants.

"What the fuck happened?" he asked, turning to his brother. He gingerly touched his nose—which looked broken—and winced. He looked at Lottie. "Holy shit, girl! What happened to your neck? You're bleeding like a stuck pig!" His gaze flashed from side to side. "Are we in the cemetery?" He turned back to Xavier. "Am I fucking drunk or something?"

"Or something."

"Well, shit." He looked back at Lottie. "Damn, girl, this place is bad luck for you." After patting his pocket, he pulled out a cell phone. "You look like you got your hands full," he said to Xavier. "I'll call for an ambulance and have them meet us out front. Can you get her out there?"

"Yes."

Julien once again looked at Lottie and then touched his nose and made a face. He shook his head. "I don't know if I want to know what happened."

"You don't," Xavier told him.

"Fair enough." He turned and jogged from sight.

Finally, Lottie's brain felt like it was beginning to solidify even if the rest of her body still felt like jelly. "Sanite?" she asked Xavier.

"Yeah. I suspected for a while." His smile was like heaven to her eyes. "I know we have a lot to discuss, but save your energy. Let's get you all patched up and then we'll talk."

She nodded and for the first time felt the pain of

the cut on her neck. Closing her eyes, she leaned her forehead against the curve of his chest. It was the last thing she remembered.

CHAPTER TWENTY-TWO

Lottie was pretty sure someone had replaced the pudding that had been filling her head for the last couple of days with nails. Or maybe knives. At least the sharpness of the pain was a welcome reprieve from dull, confused, and dazed. Although she definitely felt those last two as she blinked rapidly into the bright lights of whatever room she was in.

Grimacing, she touched her head. "Where am I?"

"Emergency room."

Once her eyes focused that became obvious. Xavier sat in a chair beside her looking...grim. She didn't like seeing that expression on his gorgeous face.

"You know, I'm really sick of waking up disoriented and not knowing where I am." She paused. "I wonder if that's how Sam feels," she added lightly and then realized how awful that came out. She shot him a quick, apologetic glance. "Sorry, that was mean."

He shrugged. "Sam's hardly my favorite person. I'm sure it's well deserved."

It was just the two of them in the exam room. "So, what's going on?"

"Good news, you are now the proud recipient of eleven stitches."

"Yay," she said dully.

"The bad news, the doctor wasn't about to let me take you out of here until you woke up. I think he wants to ask you a few questions about what happened."

"What did you tell him?"

"You fell and cut yourself on a broken bottle."

"Good call. It'd be a little hard to explain the ghost of a woman who died in the 19th century, acting through your brother, decided to slit my throat." She kept her words breezy in the hope of erasing the scowl on his face. It only deepened. "Did the doctor believe your story?"

"Not a chance."

"Well, I'm awake. I guess I'm ready to answer some questions."

He rose. "I'll get the nurse—"

A knock on the door stopped him. The doctor peeked into the room, his eyes immediately settling on her. "Oh good. You're up." Stepping into the room, he said to Xavier, "If you don't mind, I'd like to speak to Miss Boyd alone."

"He can stay," she interjected just as he rose.

"Don't worry about it. I'll go."

Lottie had a hard time believing he would just walk out of the room. It seemed so out of character. But he did. The door closed behind him with a thunk that made her cringe.

She needed to get out of the hospital and figure out what was going on, and fast. Thankfully, the knives in her head allowed for more agile brain response than pudding.

"It's good to see you again Dr. Anderson," she

said cheerily. "We didn't get much of a chance to talk the other night. You left in such a hurry."

"I, um, yes..."

"No fence this time. But I am such a klutz. I swear, my two left feet are going to kill me some day. Stupid beer bottles." For emphasis, she touched the bandage on her neck and made a face. The wound throbbed dully under her fingers. Numbing agent must be wearing off.

"Miss Boyd..."

She jumped off the table, ignoring her brain as it sloshed around in her skull. "So, that's it, right? Can I go?"

His lips pursed together.

"I assume you still have all my insurance stuff. You know, since I was here the other night."

"Yes, but..."

"Good. Hopefully, I won't be back. In fact, I'm pretty sure I won't be. Whatever bad luck was cursing me is over. Would you mind telling Armand Laroque that when you see him again? Tell him, 'The mystery is solved.'"

The doctor nodded roughly, a stricken expression on his face. "Miss Boyd, I'd really rather you didn't mention seeing me at *Luxure* to anyone."

"I can do that. You do have my discharge papers...?"

The implied blackmail wasn't lost on him. He scribbled something on a paper and handed it to her as well as a prescription for pain pills.

"Thanks, Dr. Anderson. You've been a big help."

Shockingly, Xavier wasn't waiting for her in the hall. He *was* in the lobby and moved to meet her when she emerged from the hall. But his body language was off. *He* seemed off.

239

"We're good," she told him.

He nodded. "I'll grab a cab while you check out."

Baffled, she watched him walk away. He was just so…distant. A pit opened in her stomach and she did her best to ignore it.

She spent a few minutes at the nurse's station before retrieving her prescription and then heading out into the humid night air. Despite the mild temperature, she felt chilled, like her body would never be warm again. It might have something to do with the miniscule amount of clothes on her body but she doubted it.

She still felt somewhat jumbled. And her body still reeled from, well, everything. But she was starting to come back to herself. Xavier's cool demeanor didn't help though.

He was leaning against the cab when she approached, opening the door for her but not saying a word. Just as silently she climbed inside.

Something was definitely wrong. She could tell by the way his lips pressed into a tight line.

Maybe she'd misinterpreted his gestures, his feelings. Just because he was nice to her, just because he was protective, just because he seemed finely attuned to her needs, just because they'd made love, didn't mean he wanted to put up with her shit long term. This could have simply been a roller-coaster ride for him—as it had been for her—but one he was now ready to exit.

She tried not to think about it as he closed the passenger door and walked around to the other side of the cab. Pulling her knees up to her chest, she wrapped her arms tightly around them and curled her body into the nook joining the door and seat.

Climbing in beside her, he took one look her

direction and sighed. After giving the cabbie his address, he leaned back in his seat and closed his eyes.

The pit in her stomach deepened. Anxious to reconnect with him, anxious to affirm their common bond, she asked, "Do you think it's really over?" after a few moments of awkward silence.

"I hope so," he replied, keeping his eyes closed.

"I mean, we saw Élise, we know that she's…" She glanced at the cabbie. Chatting on his cell phone, he wasn't paying them any attention. "In heaven, or whatever, but what about Sanite? What about the curse?"

"I'd like to think it's broken. I have to believe it is."

"But she's still here."

"I'd venture to guess spirits are around us every day. She might have been one of the more powerful ones, but I think I know how to knock some of the wind out of her sails. You know the altars? That's where spirits get their power. Through the gifts we give them. I believe that's how Laurent was able to communicate with me. My family's been giving Sanite too much power over the years. I'm taking her altar down."

She nodded. Why did he keep his eyes closed? She couldn't read him if she couldn't look at him.

"Why didn't Élise just come out and tell me what to do? I think I'd rather have been spared living such a sad memory."

Finally he turned to her, his eyes distant. "I get it. But I don't know that it works that way. Besides, would you have believed her?"

"No. I guess not. She did try to force me, early on. It just scared me more than anything."

"Right. She needed you to understand. To know

241

exactly what happened. And like I said earlier, I don't know that ghosts can communicate with us directly."

"She was able to use the water as conduit. Like when I heard her voice in the shower, or later when I took a bath. The water must have had power for her because she drowned." Just the thought of it, the memory of living it, made her heart ache. It was still too much to process. "What about Julien?" she asked after a moment. The cab was turning onto his street.

"Possessed by Sanite. I'm sure of it."

"I know, but how do we know it won't happen again?"

"I talked to him on the way to the hospital. I explained everything. He was shocked, and I'd like to think appalled, but he seemed to understand everything. I really do think it's over, Lottie."

The cab pulled over. As he paid the cabbie, she cracked her door and climbed out. Wrapping her arms tightly around her chest, she waited for him on the cold sidewalk.

He took one look at her and made a face. "C'mon," he said, taking her elbow and turning her toward the gated courtyard entrance. Let's get you to the Guest House before you break a leg."

For a brief moment, his joke made her hopeful everything really was okay and he was just as exhausted as she was. But his touch felt all wrong. For the first time, it felt…stiff. Forced.

Once inside the suite, things immediately got awkward.

She stood before him, one arm wrapped tight against her chest as she gripped the opposite elbow while he silently watched. He made no attempts to reach for her, no signs that he wanted to touch her at all. She needed to say something, to ask if they were okay, but uttering the words were terrifying. What if he confirmed her fears? That the ride was over for him. Whatever bond she thought they'd shared shattered when the mystery of Élise Cantrelle was solved.

"I'm going to take care of that altar," he said. "You okay for a bit?"

"Sure. I could probably stand to wash off this fresh layer of blood and dirt."

"Okay." He reached for the door.

His body was halfway into the other room when she called his name. He ducked his head back in.

"Are you coming back?"

"Do you want me to?"

She felt her brows push together. "Yes."

"Then I will." The door clicked softly behind him.

He'd been so caring in the cemetery. What happened?

Grabbing some fresh clothes, she shuffled to the bathroom and tried to piece together the last ten hours. It was such an emotional blur, a smorgasbord of chaotic events and mental time travel. Everything had been good up until *Luxure*. Then after he'd carried her home and…

Oh God, she'd seduced him. While he'd tried to push her away.

Was that what he was upset about?

She had little desire to climb back into the bathtub after everything that had happened there, so she used a washcloth and the vanity sink to wash the grime from her body.

The chicken feet dangling from the showerhead caught her eye, a towel now draped over them. Obviously, Xavier had covered them. Probably when he'd drawn the bath, probably to spare her from having to gaze upon their grossness.

In spite of everything, it made her smile. Just another example of his endless sweet gestures. The things that man had done for her...to her...

She was shocked she could feel so deeply for someone in such a short amount of time. And completely terrified. But there it was, staring directly at her.

She might be scared of what would happen if he rejected her, but she had to admit she was also scared of what would happen if he didn't. Eventually, she pushed everyone away. Why should he be any different?

Because she wanted him to be different. Because of everything they'd shared. Because Élise's heartbreaking tale had reminded her life is short, and no opportunity for happiness should be passed by. No matter how fleeting.

But knowing, wanting, and doing were three different things.

She had to tell him how she felt. In the end it didn't matter how he felt, or whether or not he wanted to be with her. He deserved to know how much he meant to her. He deserved a lot more than that.

As soon as he returned she'd spill everything.

If her heart didn't explode between now and then.

CHAPTER TWENTY-THREE

Ignoring the trepidation on Lottie's face and body language that clearly said, "Stay away from me", Xavier headed straight for Sanite's altar. He'd get to the bottom of her apprehension. He knew what he wanted. He needed to hear her desires. But first he needed to take care of his crazy great-aunt. It was the only way he'd feel safe with Lottie in the house.

The first thing he did was extinguish the freshly lit candles. Setting Sanite's portrait on the adjacent shelf, he dumped the contents of her basket into Laurent's before moving the statues into a closet. He was in the middle of filling a trash bag with the remaining items scattered on the table when Grandmere's shriek and grip on his arm interrupted him.

"What do you think you're doing, boy?"

Even though she was blind, he was pretty sure she knew exactly what he was doing.

"Taking away a little power from Aunt Sanite," he said without pausing in the clean-up.

"You can't do that." Her voice was almost a growl. "She'll be very angry."

Letting the bag ease from his hand, he slowly turned to her, afraid of what he might see. "And so...what?"

"She is a powerful Voodoo queen." Her face was twisted into a snarl.

"Was, you mean," he said quietly. The snarl deepened. "Was. She's dead."

That same low growl erupted in her throat, her clouded eyes flashed black and she lunged at him, her wrinkled hands clawing at his face. She was stronger than she should be, and he struggled to keep her at bay without hurting her.

"You had to bring that girl here!" she screeched. "You were warned, but like every man, you couldn't resist a pretty girl, could you!"

He let her back him against the shelf. His hand braced against her sternum, he was able to keep her at arm's length, but not without sacrificing his forearms. She clawed at scratched at them, blood seeping from his skin. He didn't dare push her away. If she happened to fall…

Holy shit. This wasn't quite what he expected. He wasn't sure the day could get any weirder.

Reaching over his shoulder, he fumbled for the portrait. She continued to thrash against his outstretched arm, a series of inhuman noises erupting from her.

Fingers skimming the edge, he barely secured his grasp on the frame before jerking his arm over her head and smashing the portrait into the wall. Glass shattered, Grandmere shrieked, the room seemed to shudder, and then the old woman went limp.

He jumped forward to catch her before she toppled over, easing her to the floor.

Her clouded eyes blinked at him as her chest

heaved. "I told you that girl wouldn't be welcome in this house," she whispered, her voice sounding strained. "I told you you'd make her angry."

"Are you all right?" he asked, shaking off the shock of her apparent possession and subsequent attack.

She nodded. "What happened? Did I hurt you?"

He glanced at his scratched forearms. "I'll heal."

The snarl returned, but this time it was just her normal petulant expression. She nodded again. "Help me to my feet."

"I'm taking Sanite's altar down," he told her as he lifted her from the floor.

"That's a bad idea."

"It's what has to happen."

"It won't change nothin'. Do not, under any circumstances, underestimate her. You must respect her, even fear her. You must trust me on this, boy. Even in death she has power."

"I'm well aware of that. She tried to kill Lottie."

If she was shocked by his words she didn't show it. "I did warn you."

He could hardly believe his ears. It was implausible that the woman before him, the matriarch of his family, the woman who had helped raise him, could be so callous.

"So you knew all along! You knew Sanite had cursed Élise Cantrelle and her family, and you did nothing!"

"I don't know nothin' about no curse." Her jaw squared defiantly.

He had to trust her. If he didn't, his entire existence would seem like a fraud. "What do you know, Grandmere?" he asked, forcing his tone to soften.

247

She lifted her chin. "Élise Cantrelle killed Laurent Villere, Sanite's brother, and your grandfather. She nearly destroyed this family." The words were almost said with pride.

"Hardly. Laurent was in love with Élise. He was killed by a jealous American man. Shot in the chest as he left Élise's house."

Grandmere's eyes narrowed. "How do you know these things?"

"I've been living them in dreams, through the eyes of a Loa, through Laurent's spirit. The same as Lottie, only through Élise's eyes."

Her blind eyes widened.

"I really don't have time to explain right now, but this is what's going to happen, from now on there will be no shrines made for her. Not even a small one—"

"But without her, this family, this house, our legacy, would be nothing. Nothing!"

"And we can still pay our respects, Grandmere, without giving her spirit more power. You said it yourself, she is dangerous. Look what just happened. She is jealous and she is resentful. Of a woman her brother loved. A woman who did nothing but love him back. Why would you want to empower her?"

"She is our legacy..."

"And so is Laurent!"

"I realize that, boy, but—"

"But nothing!" It was the firmest tone he'd ever taken with her and she shrank back a little. "I love you, Grandmere, and my eyes have finally been opened to the truth of Voodoo, of everything you're tried to teach me for years, but this is the way it is going to be. Not only did Sanite nearly kill the woman I love, but she almost got Julien killed in the process. She nearly destroyed *this* family. Now, today. And she destroyed Lottie's family. Her reign is over."

He shoved the remaining altar items, including the tablecloth, into the bag and tied it tight. Grabbing Sanite's shattered portrait, he stooped and kissed Grandmere's cheek. Though her jaw was still firmly clamped shut, she didn't fight him. "Call on Papa Legba. Ask Grandpere. You will see the truth."

He left her standing in the store. There would more time to explain to her and to his mother, who he was pretty sure was already on his side. Right now, he needed to get back to Lottie.

After locking the items from Sanite's altar in the safe, that was exactly what he did.

Lottie was still wrestling with her own demons and insecurity when three knocks sounded from the door.

"Hey," Xavier whispered when she opened the door. "May I come in?"

She opened it wide. "Of course."

His expression was still reserved. That couldn't be a good sign.

She shut the door softly behind him.

He walked all the way into the room, seemingly surveying his surroundings before turning to her. "How's your neck?"

She subconsciously touched the bandage and then dropped her hand. "Good." She was hoping he'd reach for her as he had so many times before, anxious for his touch, anxious for reassurance she was right about his feelings. Anxious to be close.

When he stood rigid, her body immediately began to fidget. Heat rose in her belly and her heart began to beat at a frenzied pace.

"I think I took care of any problems we might have here. You can feel safe staying."

Did that mean he wanted her to stay or he was saying she could stay until she booked her ass home?

"So, what now?" she asked instead, too afraid to be direct. Her earlier internal speech about telling him how she felt was drowned out by the roaring of blood in her ears.

"You tell me."

Oh God. What did that mean?

She was trying to organize her haphazard thoughts into cohesion when he said, "I need to ask you something and I want you to be honest."

She nodded rapidly, dismissing the pain it caused in her neck. The heat in her body rose and she could feel sweat begin to bead on her skin.

"Now that all of this...shit is over..." He paused and took a deep breath, settling his dark gaze directly on her. "I'm just going to come out and say it. Lottie, when you kiss me do you think of Laurent?"

She blinked. "What?"

"When you're with me, is it Laurent you're thinking of?"

"Is that what you think?"

"Well, you *were* all over me after the séance and then after *Luxure*... I think it's a legitimate question." Shaking his head, he looked away.

Run, a tiny voice said in her head.

"You really think I'm that desperate? That lonely? That delusional?"

He turned back, his expression...appalled. "No. It's just...after all the crazy shit that's happened, I don't know *what* to believe. I can't trust my own instincts any more."

Runrun.

Her body was on fire. Panic seized her chest, squeezing tight with every rapid beat. "So you let me seduce you...you had *sex* with me...all the while believing I was only with you because of Laurent?"

Runrunrun.

The fear and panic still squeezing her heart tight crept over her skin. She couldn't handle it, this, any of it. It was delusional for her to think she could. She had to get away, get out before things got worse. One more heartbreak was likely to send her over the edge.

Runrunrunrunrunrunrun!

Diving for her suitcase, she frantically stuffed the escaped clothing and toiletries back inside.

"Whoa, what are you doing?"

"What does it look like I'm doing, Xavier. It's over. Élise is free, the curse is broken, and I have a chance of living a full fucking life—if I can make it to the stupid airport without killing myself in the process."

"It's one a.m..."

"Maybe there's a red-eye. Or I'll just rent a car. "

"Lottie…"

She shook her head. "No."

"Look at me."

She shook her head again. Zipping her case closed, she started for the door when he took her arm. "Damnit, Lottie, stop!"

She couldn't. If she hesitated one second she'd be lost. It was better to leave now while her emotions were mostly intact. If she could be alone, she might actually be able to process them.

Yanking her arm free, she bolted out the door and down the steps, her roller clanging behind her.

Xavier was steps away. He caught up to her in the

courtyard, jerking her around so quickly it jolted her back into him. He held her tightly as her suitcase flopped onto the ground beside them.

"Just stop!" he yelled, still holding her. "You are making me crazy. Quit running away. Look, I didn't mean to upset you. Seriously. Jesus!" He took a deep breath. "I just needed to make sure your feelings for me were real and not because of some fucking dream or vision or possession or ghosts or some other weird shit."

His embrace felt so good. She closed her eyes, her body shaking so violently it felt like pieces of her would start breaking off.

"Of course they're real," she said into his chest, her voice shuddering with the effort. She might have pulled away but he held her tight. "Why wouldn't they be?"

Finally, he eased backward, still keeping her shoulders gripped in his hands. "Okay." He bowed his head to look at her. "Okay?"

Stay, the voice murmured in her head.

She continued to shake, fighting back tears. She was done with crying. She was too exhausted to cry. She was too exhausted to think.

"I don't know."

Stay, it whispered. *Stay.*

His sigh was audible. "I know you've been through a lot. I know you're still probably confused. But you've got to help me understand. Please?"

She shook her head fiercely. She couldn't answer him. Couldn't say a word from the emotion threatening to overwhelm her. It was the cemetery all over again.

Just breathe.

"All right, then I'll start. I want to be with you,

Lottie. And not because of Élise or Laurent or any of that. And I'm sorry I doubted you or your intentions. It's just all been a little...overwhelming." He smiled softly. "Look, I know you have to finish out this semester, but after I would really like to see where this goes."

She heaved air in and out of her lungs in an attempt to convince her brain to relax.

"Me too," she finally squeaked out. She took a few more deep breaths to try to regain some of her senses, to calm the panic. She could do this. She needed to do this.

"I think you belong here," he continued. "In New Orleans, with me."

His expression was so sincere it was hard to understand why her heart was filled with so much doubt.

"But I need to know that you want it, too. That you want me."

God, what had she—?

"I do!" she blurted. "I've wanted you from the start."

"Good. Good," he repeated, bending to softly press his lips to hers.

In an instant, all ounces of anxiety, doubt, fear, and panic drained from her body, eased by the passion in his touch, the love in his hands. More than that, it was chased away by emotions far more powerful than fear or doubt. It was the overwhelming sensation of feeling like she finally belong somewhere and hopefully...with someone.

EPILOGUE

The room still smelled like paint, and the lavender candles Xavier had lit to help cover the smell just made it smell like lavender scented paint. It would have to do.

The room was supposed to be remodeled weeks ago but the contractor flaked out, so it had just been finished this morning. He would have put Lottie up in the suite again, but couldn't. Since they hadn't made their Jazz Fest deadline and it had been booked months ago, he couldn't stand to lose the income.

He'd rather just have her stay with him. But things were still weird with Grandmere. He knew she didn't actually have anything against Lottie, but she was deathly afraid of Sanite and definitely worried about her wrath.

He could understand. Luckily, there hadn't been any evidence his long-deceased aunt was still hanging around. Hopefully, that wouldn't change when Lottie got here since her apartment wouldn't be ready for a couple of weeks.

Her flight was scheduled to land in a couple of hours. He hadn't been so anxious for someone's arrival since his estranged father promised to come to his tenth birthday party. He hadn't, of course, but Xavier's ten-year-old self hadn't been able to sleep he'd been so excited.

It was still hard to believe the path that had brought him here, but he wouldn't change a moment of it if it meant he didn't meet Lottie. And not only did he gain her, his eyes were opened to a heritage he'd spent a lot of energy trying to deny. Although, he had to admit he was still coming to terms with it.

To think, for years, Laurent Villere tried to communicate with him via the one repeating dream, all because Xavier liked to toss a few coins into an altar basket for good luck. But there was a reason Voodoo was now synonymous with unexplainable.

In fact, if he hadn't witnessed every crazy thing that had happened firsthand—from the dreams, to Julien's possession, to the giant skull taking Élise to the afterworld, to his grandmother viciously attacking him—he'd be the first one to commit himself to a mental hospital.

He looked at the time again. Shit, still two hours. He wasn't sure how he was going to get through the afternoon without wearing a path on the carpet from pacing.

Soft knocking sounded on the hotel door. Brow furrowed, he went to answer it. He wasn't expecting anyone, obviously, but it might be a guest, or perhaps his mother or Grandmere needed something.

What greeted him when he opened the door was even better. Lottie stood before him, looking radiant in a breezy cotton dress, a beaming smile on her beautiful face.

Throwing her arms around his neck, she jumped into his arms and wrapped her legs around his waist.

"I couldn't wait to see you. I caught the earliest flight I could," she said before devouring him with a kiss.

It wouldn't have ended until both of them were naked, sweaty, and satiated, but Xavier caught a glimpse of his brother walking from the courtyard. Julien had been...different since Sanite's possession, but he still didn't trust him around Lottie.

Reluctantly, he broke their kiss. "What the hell is Julien—"

Lottie's tongue interrupted him. Doubts about Julien were tossed aside as his brain turned to other matters, namely his hands cupping her smooth, bare thighs. Maybe naked had been presumptuous. He could just slide her panties aside...

Kicking the door closed with his foot, he headed for the bed.

It was Lottie who pulled back this time. Lip caught between her teeth, she wore a sly smile. "Happy to see me?"

"Can't you tell?"

Her hips rocked against his pelvis. "So, those aren't wooden stakes you're packing?"

"Not today."

Her neck looked like it needed attention. "I do wish you'd called me," he murmured between tracing the curve of her throat with his tongue. "I'd have picked you up at the airport."

"That's okay. I wanted to surprise you. Julien picked me up."

He paused mid-neck nibble to look at her. "What?"

"I thought it would be a good idea to clear the air." She offered him a smile and a soft kiss. "It was nice. We had a pleasant conversation and he even apologized for everything, even though we know he wasn't acting of his own free will."

Julien was definitely different all right.

Her undulating hips brought his mind back to more important things.

"Your jeans look a little binding," she said. "Why don't we get you out of them and into something more comfortable. Namely me."

"Gladly."

Easing her back onto the bed, he couldn't believe how perfect this felt. There was no denying she belonged here, in New Orleans, with him.

Coming Soon in 2014!

Bayou Grisé
A follow up to Villere House

<u>Other Books by C.D. Hussey</u>

The Human Vampire Series
La Luxure: **Discover Your Blood Lust**
Book One in the Human Vampire Series
de Sang: **Embrace Your Blood Lust**
Book Two in the Human Vampire Series
Eveillez: **Deny Your Blood Lust**
Book Three in the Human Vampire Series
Expiez: **Redeem Your Blood Lust**
Book Four in the Human Vampire Series

Contemporary Romance
Unexpected Oasis
Coming Soon!

To stay updated with C.D. Hussey, please visit:
http://www.cdhussey.com/

If you would like stay connected with Leslie Fear,
below are a few links to her social media pages:
https://www.facebook.com/author.leslie.fear
https://www.goodreads.com/author/show/7202737.Leslie_Fear
http://www.theindiebookshelf.com/search/label/leslie%20fear
http://jilliandodd.net/category/leslies-book-bliss

ABOUT THE AUTHORS

When not writing, C.D. Hussey enjoys a career as a professional engineer. She currently lives in the Midwest with her husband, teenage son and two cats. With an ongoing love affair with New Orleans, expect to see her in the Crescent City at least twice a year.

Leslie Fear began writing as a stay-at-home-mom and has two unfinished novels she'd like to return to someday. In addition, her love for reading lead to reviewing books for Goodreads and Amazon and also co-founding The Indie Bookshelf blog. She also enjoys her work as review contributor for author, Jillian Dodd's blog.

Leslie lives in Texas with her husband, teenage son and daughter and one very silly pug.

Made in the USA
San Bernardino, CA
06 July 2018